GETTING ACQUAINTED

"You all right, ma'am?" Clint asked.

"Yes," Lynn replied. "I . . . I just . . ."

"Shut your goddamn mouth!" Mark roared. "I'll deal with you when I'm through with this one!"

Clint held his ground and waited for Mark to collect his courage. When Mark finally did make another move, Clint saw it coming as clearly as if he'd watched a bank of storm clouds roll over in the course of a day.

Mark's first swing was rushed and was announced by a grunting breath as well as a shift in his entire body. All Clint needed to do was take a step back to allow that punch to miss him by a foot. Mark's second swing was a bit faster, but Clint was able to see it coming in enough time to spare for him to slap it away. When Mark bared his teeth and let out a frustrated obscenity, it was almost funny.

Clint took hold of Mark's shirt and held him at arm's length. Before Mark could respond, Clint punched him in the face with a straight right jab. As Clint's knuckles cracked against Mark's chin, Clint knew he hadn't hit the other man hard enough to do any more than catch his attention.

"I'll buy the first drink," Clint said. "No need to keep tussling if there's no call for it."

"Oh, there's a call for it," Mark replied before lunging forward and throwing a punch intended to turn Clint's face into strawberry jam.

THE GUNSMITH

311

TO REAP AND TO SOW

J. R. ROBERTS

JOVE BOOKS, NEW YORK

THE BERKLEY PUBLISHING GROUP
Published by the Penguin Group
Penguin Group (USA) Inc.
375 Hudson Street, New York, New York 10014, USA
Penguin Group (Canada), 90 Eglinton Avenue East, Suite 700, Toronto, Ontario M4P 2Y3, Canada
(a division of Pearson Penguin Canada Inc.)
Penguin Books Ltd., 80 Strand, London WC2R 0RL, England
Penguin Group Ireland, 25 St. Stephen's Green, Dublin 2, Ireland (a division of Penguin Books Ltd.)
Penguin Group (Australia), 250 Camberwell Road, Camberwell, Victoria 3124, Australia
(a division of Pearson Australia Group Pty. Ltd.)
Penguin Books India Pvt. Ltd., 11 Community Centre, Panchsheel Park, New Delhi—110 017, India
Penguin Group (NZ), 67 Apollo Drive, Rosedale, North Shore 0632, Auckland, New Zealand
(a division of Pearson New Zealand Ltd.)
Penguin Books (South Africa) (Pty.) Ltd., 24 Sturdee Avenue, Rosebank, Johannesburg 2196,
South Africa

Penguin Books Ltd., Registered Offices: 80 Strand, London WC2R 0RL, England

This is a work of fiction. Names, characters, places, and incidents either are the product of the author's imagination or are used fictitiously, and any resemblance to actual persons, living or dead, business establishments, events, or locales is entirely coincidental.

TO REAP AND TO SOW
A Jove Book / published by arrangement with the author

PRINTING HISTORY
Jove edition / November 2007

ISBN: 978-0-515-14372-0

JOVE®
Jove Books are published by The Berkley Publishing Group,
a division of Penguin Group (USA) Inc.,
375 Hudson Street, New York, New York 10014.
JOVE is a registered trademark of Penguin Group (USA) Inc.
The "J" design is a trademark belonging to Penguin Group (USA) Inc.

PRINTED IN THE UNITED STATES OF AMERICA

10 9 8 7 6 5 4 3 2 1

ONE

The palm of Mark Rowlett's hand made a sound that filled the room as it slapped across Lynn McKay's face. It wasn't a very big room, so most any sound would echo inside of it, but the slap had a jarring ring to it that silenced all the other shouting that had come before.

Lynn was a tall woman in her early twenties with a slender build and long blond hair. The elegant lines of her face were contorted into a stark expression of surprise as she placed her hand upon her face where the sting of that slap was still very much alive.

"You hit me," Lynn whispered.

Mark Rowlett was a big fellow who stood only a few inches taller than Lynn. His mouth hung open to reveal uneven rows of dirty teeth. Every breath he took rustled the whiskers that covered the entire lower half of his face. "Yer damn right I hit you," he snarled. "You had it comin' for what you did."

"I didn't do anything! That's what I keep trying to tell you!"

Although she'd been standing up to him until now, Lynn flinched when she saw Mark make a move toward her.

Mark grinned at the sight of that. He picked up on her

little show of weakness the way a circling vulture picked up on a rabbit that had been lying still for just a bit too long.

"Don't give me that bullshit," Mark grunted. "I know what a whore like you does when I ain't around to keep an eye on you."

Someone knocked on the door, but Mark ignored it. He stood in the little hotel room with his back to the door so he could glare at everything else in the room. For the most part, he focused upon Lynn, who turned so she could look into a small round shaving mirror hanging from a hook over a washbasin.

As much as Lynn wanted to cry, she kept herself from doing it. She knew Mark would enjoy that sight a bit too much. Steeling herself as she gingerly touched her cheek, Lynn said, "That's probably the owner telling you to stop making so much noise."

"Well, he can go to hell!" Mark shouted as he turned toward the door.

Despite the curse, whoever was outside the room knocked again. Mark grinned wider, bowed out his chest a bit and pulled open the door as if he was about to accept an award.

Standing in the hallway was a slender man who was Lynn's height. He wore a rumpled vest and a white shirt with sleeves rolled up to reveal a pair of arms that looked more like twigs hanging from his shoulders. "Is there a problem in there?" the man asked in a grating voice.

"Nah," Mark replied. "Thanks for askin', though."

"If you two wouldn't mind keeping it down . . . I'd surely appreciate it."

"Yeah? Well I'd appreciate you leaving us alone. I paid for this room and I'll do what I please whilst I'm in it."

The man in the vest laced his fingers together and rubbed the sweat from his palms back into his skin. "I know," he mumbled, "but there are other guests and—"

Mark cut the man off by slamming the door in his face.

He stayed there and chuckled as if he could see the reaction he'd gotten from the skinny man outside.

"Good, Mark," Lynn said. "That's real good."

"Little weasel should've kept his mouth shut. Just like you should've kept your legs closed."

Lynn rolled her eyes and dabbed a wet cloth on her red cheek. "First of all, we're not married and we never will be. You don't have a claim on me or what I do. Second of all, I didn't do anything."

"Then why'd you gussy yerself up and buy all that perfume?"

For a moment, Lynn stood there as if waiting for Mark to finish his sentence. When she realized he was done, she shook her head and said, "I don't believe you. I bought some perfume with my own money and—"

"And who d'you wanna smell so good for?" Mark snapped.

"It sure as hell isn't you."

Reflexively, Mark took another swing at her. This time, however, Lynn was ready for him. She stepped to one side and ducked down, which was more than enough to get out of his line of fire. The momentum of Mark's fist swung through the air carried him to the table that held the washbasin.

He let out a snarling yell as his fist knocked into the basin and sent it clanging to the floor. When he stopped to take a breath, Mark heard more knocking coming from the door. He turned on his heels and pulled the door open to find the man in the vest standing there again.

"Sir, I'll have to insist you keep it down," the skinny man said. "Otherwise, I'll have to bring the law in here to settle this."

"You'll what?" Mark growled as he lunged from the room to grab hold of the skinny man by his lapels.

Lynn's eyes widened, but she was pleased to see the skinny man hold his ground. Even though the man was squirming within his vest, he did a fairly good job of keeping his chin up.

"I can't allow this sort of behavior in my hotel," the skinny man said. "Especially when it's against a woman."

Mark tightened his grip on the other man's shirt and pulled the fellow closer while leaning in to growl, "You don't get to tell me what to do, especially where this woman's concerned."

"It . . . it's not just me, sir. There's been complaints from other guests."

"Then let 'em complain. All of you can go to hell." With that, Mark snapped both arms out and sent the skinny man slamming back into the door across the hall. This time, Mark admired his work directly instead of staring at a closed door.

"I hope he does bring the law in here," Lynn said. "That way, you can go to jail for being such an asshole."

Although Mark felt Lynn's fist bounce off his shoulder, it wasn't enough to tarnish the smile he wore. Mark continued his slow turn as he shut the door and faced Lynn. The anger etched into her features only made him smile more.

"He won't call in the law," Mark said. "Just like you won't do a goddamn thing besides get that dress off and lie down."

Lynn froze until she started to shake her head in bewilderment. "You think I'm going to do anything with you after this?"

"Sure. That perfume you bought smells real good." When he saw she wasn't moving, Mark added, "You mean you already got your fill from whoever else you opened your legs for?"

Still shaking her head, Lynn told him, "I didn't do anything with anyone else and I sure as hell won't be doing anything with you. Not anymore."

"What? Because of that little slap? You hit me plenty of times!"

"And you barely felt it. You would have knocked me out if I hadn't ducked out of the way."

"And now we'll put things straight. You wanna smooth this over, we can do it right now. Come on, I know how you like it."

"You don't even know how to keep your pecker straight for more than two minutes at a time," Lynn chuckled.

The smirk on Mark's face remained intact, but an animal hunger showed in his eyes. Without a bit of warning, he lashed out with one hand to knock the washbasin's table against the wall. With his next swing, he threw Lynn onto the bed. "I'll show you just what I mean, bitch."

Someone knocked on the door.

The instant he heard that, Mark turned and pulled it open. When he didn't see the man in the vest standing outside, he stared with slack-jawed surprise.

"Hey there," Clint Adams said. "You mind keeping it down?"

TWO

"Who the hell are you?" Mark grunted.

Clint leaned to one side so he could see past Mark and into the room. "I'm one of the guests that have been complaining about the noise," he replied. "I heard the owner mention that a few minutes ago."

"Yeah?"

After seeing Lynn climbing off the bed and rubbing the bruised portion of her face, Clint shifted his eyes back toward Mark. "Yeah," he said while staring the man down. "And I think you need to step outside to cool yourself off."

"Why don't you step outside, mister?"

"So you can toss a woman around some more?" Clint shook his head. "I don't think so. There's a saloon across the street. Why don't you go there and leave the lady alone?"

"Go to hell, asshole. I'll do what I please with this bitch. You want some for yourself, you can wait around for your turn like everyone else."

Mark was still grinning when he felt a tap on his shoulder. As he glanced behind him to look toward Lynn, it was obvious that he intended on giving her a moment to try to appease him. What he got instead was something very different.

Lynn glared at him defiantly and snapped her right hand around so quickly that Mark was unable to avoid getting slapped. Her palm landed flush against his face and did a real good job of wiping away the smug grin that had nested there for so long.

Unfortunately, Mark's surprise didn't last long. Wheeling around, he balled up his fists and let out a vicious snarl. "You're finished now, you whore!"

Bringing up his left arm, Mark sent Lynn backward with a quick shove. He took some more time to prepare his right arm, though, by cocking it back to deliver a solid punch. When he tried to unleash the punch, he found it impossible to budge his arm.

"What the hell?" Mark muttered as he tried to move his right arm.

Clint had reached out to grab Mark's arm so quickly that there was no way for Mark to do anything about it. Clint's grip was strong enough to keep Mark where he was, no matter how much Mark struggled against him.

"I believe you've been asked to leave," Clint said calmly. "It's time for you to take us up on that offer."

Mark started to say something as he brought his left fist around to punch Clint in the face, but he didn't get out more than a grunt before he felt Clint's knuckles slam into his jaw. The fast punch snapped Mark's head to the side and caused him to shift so he was facing Clint directly.

For a moment, Mark could only stand there and gawk. When he finally caught his breath, he said, "You got to the count of two before I tear your head off."

Clint stood in his spot without moving a single muscle.

As soon as he saw Mark start to throw a punch, however, Clint responded with another swing that was quick as a bolt of lightning.

"Two," Clint said after he'd delivered a sharp left hook to Mark's gut.

Doubled over and wheezing, Mark staggered back into the room.

Lynn hopped out of his way and pressed herself against a wall so she was out of both men's reach.

"You all right, ma'am?" Clint asked.

"Yes," Lynn replied. "I . . . I just . . ."

"Shut your goddamn mouth!" Mark roared. "I'll deal with you when I'm through with this one!"

Clint held his ground and waited for Mark to collect his courage. When Mark finally did make another move, Clint saw it coming as clearly as if he'd watched a bank of storm clouds roll in over the course of a day.

Mark's first swing was rushed and was announced by a grunting breath as well as a shift in his entire body. All Clint needed to do was take a step back to allow that punch to miss him by a foot. Mark's second swing was a bit faster, but Clint was able to see it coming in enough time to spare for him to slap it away. When Mark bared his teeth and let out a frustrated obscenity, it was almost funny.

Seeing the start of a grin on Clint's face was enough to push Mark into another kind of anger. He charged toward Clint and weathered a few punches on his way in before wrapping Clint up in a bear hug and shoving him against the wall that had been hit by the man in the vest not too long ago.

Clint's shoulders slammed against the door. As soon as his boots touched the floor again, he brought up one leg to slam his knee into Mark. Clint wasn't sure where the knee had landed, but it hit hard enough to loosen Mark's grip.

Clint took hold of Mark's shirt and held him at arm's length. Before Mark could respond, Clint punched him in the face with a straight right jab. As Clint's knuckles cracked against Mark's chin, Clint knew he hadn't hit the other man hard enough to do any more than catch his attention.

"I'll buy the first drink," Clint said. "No need to keep tussling if there's no call for it."

"Oh, there's call for it," Mark replied before lunging forward and throwing a punch intended to turn Clint's face into strawberry jam.

Clint shifted to the side and felt the breeze of Mark's punch sail past him. Next, Clint heard the crunching impact of Mark's fist slamming against the wall.

While Mark gritted his teeth and struggled to keep from yelping in pain, Clint positioned himself so he was standing between the man and the room where Lynn was still waiting.

Every one of Mark's haggard breaths needed to be pushed out of him. He was so angry that sweat had pumped out of his forehead and trickled down his face. The moment he got Clint back in his sights, he reached for the gun that hung in a battered holster on his hip.

Before Mark could close his fingers around his pistol, he was looking down the barrel of Clint's modified Colt.

Mark hadn't seen Clint go for his gun. He hadn't even heard Clint clear leather.

"You just lost that free drink I offered," Clint said. "Take your hand from that pistol before you lose something else."

Mark wanted to draw and fire with every fiber of his being. That much was plain to see in his eyes and the anxious twitching in his face. But no matter how worked up he was, Mark wasn't blind. He could see that he was beaten and wasn't even close to taking his own gun from its holster. Swallowing his pride along with his anger, Mark opened both hands and held them up to either side.

"Good," Clint said without shifting his aim. "Now get out of here."

Slowly, Mark backed away. "I'll be seeing you again," he grumbled.

"It's best if you don't."

   With every step he took away from Clint, Mark seemed
to grow a bit more confident. "I'll see you again. Count
on it."

   Clint watched Mark carefully without paying any mind
to the smoke he was blowing. Only when Mark turned a
corner and disappeared from the hallway did he holster the
Colt.

   "Are you all—" was all Clint managed to say before
Lynn rushed up to wrap her arms around him and plant a
kiss on his mouth that curled his toes.

THREE

Clint walked into the Red Eye Saloon later that night. After riding all day long to make it most of the way through Kansas and get into Spelling, Clint had intended on filling his stomach and climbing into bed to call it an early night. The little restaurant connected to the hotel allowed him to carry out the first part of his plan, but Mark Rowlett's shouting had cut short the second.

As he walked into the saloon, Clint didn't even make it to the bar before the short fellow tending it had locked eyes with him.

"You staying at that hotel across the street?" the bartender asked.

Clint looked around a bit just to make sure he was the one in the bartender's sights. Judging by the edge in the shorter man's voice, he must have had some pressing business to relay. Seeing that he was the intended target, Clint let out a sigh and nodded. "Yeah. I'm staying at that hotel."

"Someone was in here grousing about you."

"I suspected it might be something like that," Clint mumbled.

"Pardon?"

"Never mind. Thanks for letting me know."

Clint stepped up to the bar and rolled his head back and forth to loosen up his neck. As much as he enjoyed long rides, they played hell on him when the temperature dropped the way it had over the last few days.

The bartender leaned both hands against his edge of the bar. Now that he'd stepped up to stand directly in front of Clint, it was easy to see he was even shorter than Clint had first guessed. In fact, the bartender was standing on a crate situated behind the bar.

"You know how I knew you were the man that was being groused about?" the bartender asked with a twinkle in his eye.

Clint leaned forward to get a better look behind the bar. It wasn't just a crate set up back there for the short man, but an entire platform that covered most of the floor behind the bar and led to a ramp that would put him back onto the regular floor when he walked around the bar.

"Come on," the bartender asked as if he was about to burst. "You know how I knew?"

"No," Clint finally conceded. "How'd you know?"

Proudly, the bartender ran a finger along the side of his face and then pointed to that same spot on Clint's face. "Your scar. The man who groused about you mentioned a scar and I picked up on it right away."

Clint reflexively touched the scar on his cheek and nodded. Most of the times, he even forgot the scar was there. "Oh yeah," he said. "Real observant."

The bartender straightened his back and nodded. If his arms were a bit longer, he would have been able to pat himself on the back. "Don't worry, though. I didn't say anything."

"That's because you don't know who I am, or if that fellow wasn't just sounding off. I'm not the only man with a scar, for that matter."

With every word Clint said, the pride etched into the little man's face dimmed. Before too long, the bartender was staring at his own fingers. "I suppose you're right. What can I get you to drink?"

Even if the bartender was twice as big as him, Clint would have felt bad for raining on the man's parade like that. "Then again," Clint added as if he'd given the matter a good amount of thought, "not every person would have spotted me so quickly or from a distance that way."

The bartender shrugged.

"It's been a long day," Clint said. "I suppose I was just caught off my guard when you spotted me so quickly."

Slowly, the bartender's sly grin was rekindled. "I can see how that might startle you. How about I set you up with a free beer to make up for it?"

"That might just do the trick."

As the bartender got a mug and filled it for him, Clint looked around at the rest of the saloon. There really wasn't much to see. Apart from three other customers in the place, there were only a couple tables and a handful of chairs. It looked as if there might be a small stage in the back of the room, but that could have just been another platform for the bartender to use.

When the bartender turned around again, his smirk was back in full force. "Here you go. On the house. The first one is, anyway."

"Much obliged," Clint said as he lifted the mug and took a sip.

The brew wasn't the best he'd had, but it sure beat the swill he'd been served in Wichita. As he drank, Clint could feel the bartender eyeing him intently. Fortunately, the little man didn't wait long before talking again.

"You made an enemy in Mark Rowlett, you know," the bartender said.

"Yeah. I kind of figured."

"He's not the sort you'd want to trifle with."

"Then he shouldn't have been beating a woman."

The bartender nodded as his eyes drifted toward the

holster at Clint's side. "Well, I guess you can handle someone like Mark better than most. Still, he gets awfully particular where that woman of his is concerned. I take it you
know her as well?"

"I got her name, but that was about it."

"She's not . . . uh . . . hurt is she?"

Clint set his mug down and looked up to find the bartender watching him carefully. "Not too bad, no," Clint
replied. "She wanted to clean herself up a bit. Are you a
friend of hers, or just plain nosy?"

"I like to know what's going on so's I can spread the
word. All a part of the job, you know. Mark's fairly well
known around here. Folks'll want to know who put him in
his place."

Clint held the bartender's gaze until the little man
looked away. Considering the long day Clint had had, it
didn't take long for him to pull that off. "Maybe folks
should tend to their own affairs," Clint said with just enough
of an edge in his voice to get his point across.

The bartender held up his hands and averted his eyes.
"No offense meant. Just making conversation."

Clint had to laugh at the bartender's easy manner. "You
serve food here?" he asked.

"Sure do. I'm fixin' steak omelets tomorrow myself."

"Be sure to have one ready for me and I'll tell you all
about my run-in with Mr. Rowlett. Right now, I'd just like
to finish this beer and get to sleep."

Leaning over the bar so he could offer his hand, the barkeep said, "Sounds like a deal, Mr. . . . ."

As Clint shook the bartender's hand, he wondered if it
wouldn't be wiser to give a false name. Despite the attrac-
tiveness of that idea, he replied, "Adams."

"Tomorrow morning it is, Mr. Adams. I'll be looking
forward to the story."

Clint was glad to have appeased the bartender for the
time being just so he could drink the rest of his beer in

peace. Hopefully, the small town wouldn't be flooded with stories about the Gunsmith by morning thanks to Clint dropping his own name.

Then again, judging by the tenacity of the bartender, the little man probably knew who he was the moment Clint stepped through the door.

FOUR

Clint's eyes snapped open for what felt like the tenth time in as many minutes. As always, his hand reached for the modified Colt at his side but stopped just short of clearing leather. Unlike the other times that had happened, hadn't been awakened by a sound from outside or someone walking heavily down the hall.

He'd heard footsteps, sure enough, but not loud. When he looked at the narrow gap beneath his door, Clint saw two shadows where a set of feet were standing. Swinging his legs over the side of his bed without taking his hand away from his Colt, Clint walked across the small room and stood next to the door.

"What is it?" Clint asked.

The voice that came from the other side of the door was quiet but not as gruff as Clint was expecting.

"It's Lynn McKay," the voice said. "I'm the one from the room down the hall from yours."

When Clint pulled open the door, he caused Lynn to jump back half a step.

"Yeah," Clint said in a tired voice. "I remember you."

Lynn had her hands clasped in front of her as though she didn't know quite what else to do with them. When she looked at Clint, she kept her head at a demure angle, out of shyness, it seemed, more than anything else. No matter how much she tried to shrink herself down, however, there was no hiding the elegance of her tall, wispy frame.

"I never got a chance to say how much I appreciated what you did," she told him. After waiting a few silent moments, Lynn added, "Thank you."

"No need for that," Clint replied. "It was my pleasure."

"You didn't have to step in like that."

"Your friend was making a lot of noise and I was trying to sleep." Now that he was off his bed and looking at Lynn, it was hard for Clint to keep up his gruff demeanor. "I also don't like to hear a man pushing around a woman," he said in a much softer tone. "I hope I wasn't too late in getting there."

Lynn gave a quick wave with one hand. "I've gone through worse with Mark, but it won't be happening again. I'm through with him."

"That's good to hear. Was it a mutual decision?"

There was a bit of a flicker in Lynn's eyes, which put a small dent in her confidence, but she eventually nodded. "He's gone for now, but he might be back. It's happened plenty of times before."

"It may get worse now," Clint replied. "I'd hate to see anyone get blindsided by someone like that friend of yours."

Lynn put on a fresh smile as she took a step into Clint's room. "You're worried about me? That's sweet. But I can handle Mark. Now that he's shown his true colors, I won't make the mistake of giving him one more kind word. And don't worry about the rest of it either," she added as she propped one leg up on the small dresser next to Clint's door. "I can take care of myself just fine."

As she said that, Lynn reached down to hook her fingers along the bottom of her skirt and peel the material up over her leg. The smooth curve of her calf seemed to go on for days, and when it led up to her thigh, the view only got better. She wore a lacy garter midway between her knee and hip. Under that garter, held in place by a red ribbon, was a pearl-handled derringer.

Clint noticed the derringer, but preferred to keep his eyes on Lynn's perfectly contoured leg. She let her fingers drift along the exposed skin for a few seconds more than she needed to, just so Clint would know that she didn't mind him looking. When he looked back up to her, the smile on Lynn's face had taken on a much warmer tone.

"Do you know how to use that?" Clint asked.

Sliding her hand up farther along her leg to caress the little gun, Lynn pushed her skirt up a bit more and said, "Well, it's sure not just for show."

"You might not want to go around showing that to just anyone, though. They might get the wrong idea."

Lynn set her leg down and let her skirts fall to cover it. From there, she marched straight up to Clint and placed her hands on either side of his head. "Something tells me you've got the right idea already, but here's a little something to let you know for sure."

The first time Lynn had kissed him was a quick surprise. This time, Clint had been waiting to feel her lips on his until it seemed almost unbearable. Once he could taste her, he reflexively wrapped his arms around her so he could pull Lynn into his room and kick the door shut.

FIVE

As soon as Lynn was lifted off her feet, she wrapped her long legs around Clint and locked them tight. He could feel the muscles in her thighs gripping his torso almost hard enough to squeeze the breath out of him. Rather than carry her straight to the bed, he turned and pressed her back against a wall so he could continue the kiss she'd started.

Lynn's fingernails raked along Clint's back and shoulders. When he reached down to cup her tight, rounded backside in both hands, Clint felt a little moan rumble up from her throat to tickle his lips.

They both leaned back at the same time to catch their breath. Lynn's eyes were wide open and her breasts heaved against Clint's body. Her legs were still locked around him, so she didn't slip one bit as she wriggled against him and started pulling at the buttons of his shirt.

"You don't have to do this to thank me," Clint whispered as he struggled to keep his hands from moving along her body.

Lynn kept her eyes locked upon Clint as she untangled her legs from around him so she could support herself with one and let the other slide up and down along Clint's hip.

"The only reason I'm doing this is because I want to. I've wanted to since the moment I laid eyes on you."

When he saw Lynn lean in for another kiss, Clint took hold of her and planted his lips upon her mouth. Her lips opened to let her tongue flick into his as she pressed herself against him. Clint slid one hand along the delicate slope of her back while using the other to massage the perfect curve of her backside.

He stepped back and Lynn followed him. They kissed each other hungrily as they started ripping the clothes off of each other's body. Lynn had Clint all but undressed in a matter of seconds. He, on the other hand, had a bit more clothing to get through before he could see her naked figure.

Lynn giggled as she eased herself onto the bed so both legs dangled over the side. She stretched her arms up over her head and arched her back like a contented cat as Clint unbuttoned, unhooked and untied everything necessary to peel the dress and undergarments off of her.

It was an effort, but it was also worth every second. Clint felt like he was unwrapping one hell of a Christmas present as he peeled away layer after layer. When he was done, the only thing Lynn had on was the garter and the pearl-handled derringer. Clint lowered himself to his knees and pulled Lynn closer to the edge of the bed so he could run his lips against the silky smooth skin of her inner thigh.

Lynn draped her legs over Clint's shoulders and reached down to run her fingers through his hair. As she felt his tongue glide closer to the sensitive skin between her legs, she let out a slow, contented purr.

Clint moved both hands along Lynn's legs, savoring the feel of her smooth skin over the tight muscles beneath it. He let out a slow breath as his lips brushed against the downy hair between her thighs. When he could feel Lynn using her legs to pull him in closer, he ran his tongue straight up along the lips of her pussy.

Letting out a loud groan, Lynn arched her back again

and grabbed onto the bed with one hand. She kept the other hand on the back of Clint's head to keep him from stopping what he was doing.

After a few quick flicks of his tongue, Clint circled her little clitoris until Lynn was moaning and bucking her hips against his face. Soon, she was out of breath. She didn't even get a chance to catch her next breath before Clint stood up and moved her legs a bit further apart.

Even though she looked surprised to see him on his feet, Lynn opened her legs and even reached down to guide Clint's rigid penis into her. As Clint pushed his hips forward, Lynn kept her fingers wrapped around him so she could stroke every inch of his cock as it entered her. Lynn moved her fingers down so she could touch herself as Clint started to pump in and out.

Clint fell into a rhythm as he pumped his hips back and forth. Soon, he felt Lynn's legs wrapping around him. This time, however, she tightened her grip on him with her legs to pull him in even harder as he entered her. She would ease up a bit to allow him to pull back, only to pull him in once more.

Soon, Clint felt her tighten around him in a different way. Lynn let out a shuddering moan and leaned back onto the bed. She gripped the blankets with both hands and clenched her eyes shut as her first climax rippled through her body. When it built to its peak, her orgasm caused her pussy to grip his cock as if she never wanted him to slip out.

Once that storm had passed, Clint eased back and flipped her onto her stomach. All Lynn needed to feel was his hands upon her legs and she immediately knew what he wanted. She turned around so her back was to him as she placed her knees on the edge of the bed. From there, Lynn lowered her upper body and propped up her backside to make her buttocks seem even more perfectly rounded.

Clint took a moment to admire the view from behind her. His hands traced along the upper edge of her buttocks, all the way down to the wet lips of her pussy. As soon as his fingers found that spot between her legs, Lynn clawed at the bed and moaned softly in anticipation.

Even if Clint had wanted to wait any longer, he wouldn't have been able to pull it off. Only a few seconds had passed, but it felt as if he'd waited an eternity before guiding his cock inside of her. Once the tip of his erection was in her, Clint took hold of Lynn's hips and pulled her toward him as he pushed his hips forward. He could feel his erection growing even harder as he slipped inside of her. By the time he'd buried himself within Lynn's warm depths, Clint could feel her pussy gripping him once more.

"Oh my God," she whispered. When Clint grabbed hold of her hips and started pumping in earnest, she tried to say something else. All she could get out after a few tries was "Oh my . . . oh my God!"

Clint placed one hand on the small of her back so he could feel every little wriggle of her hips. He kept his other hand on Lynn's backside, simply because it was too soft to let go.

Lynn tossed her hair over one shoulder so she could turn and look back at Clint. Her mouth was open to let out every gasp. Those gasps turned into an excited yelp as Clint gave her rump a little playful smack. The grin on Lynn's face was all Clint needed to see to know how much she'd liked that.

Before long, Clint could feel his own pleasure building to its climax. His thrusts had become more powerful, and Lynn had her face buried in a pillow so she could cry out as much as she wanted. While she was riding the crest of her second orgasm, Lynn threw her head back and moaned to the ceiling.

Clint reached out to take hold of her hair and pulled it just enough to take up the slack. That pushed Lynn over the edge, and she was quickly in the grip of a climax that got her entire body shaking.

Once Clint let his eyes run from the tangle of her blond hair in his hands, down the curve of her back and along the slope of her buttocks, he was past the point of no return. He pumped into her a few more times, driving harder each time. Finally, he exploded inside of her until he swore he felt the floor tilt under his feet.

Clint let her go and then crawled onto the bed. Within seconds, Lynn was curled up and facing him with one leg draped over his side.

"I feel like I should be thanking you," she said. "Again."

"Don't mention it," Clint replied breathlessly.

Lynn ran her fingernails along Clint's arm and smiled in satisfaction. "I think I'll thank you anyway. That is . . . once we've caught our breath."

SIX

Spelling was a small enough town that Clint didn't have to walk far before reaching the edge of it. He took such a walk as the sun was breaking the eastern horizon the next morning. Standing with the dusty streets behind him, Clint gazed out at a stretch of wide open land and pulled in a breath of crisp air.

It was an odd time of year wedged in between the most recent cold snap of winter and the earliest wave of heat that would roll in for the spring. Actually, it was still mostly winter, but the winds were being generous, and Clint hadn't needed his thick wool coat for the last couple of weeks. As he pulled in another breath, he caught a hint of frost at the back of his throat.

It would be getting colder soon. There could possibly even be some snow before too long. This morning, though, was bright and clear. It was the kind of morning that made Clint want to sit down to a big breakfast and stuff himself with griddle cakes covered in syrup.

He had those thoughts in his head as he turned around and spotted a pair of men walking straight toward him. Clint squared his shoulders and dropped one hand to rest upon his Colt when he saw that one of those men was Mark Rowlett.

"Where's Lynn?" Mark grunted.

Clint didn't say a word. Instead, he spent the next few seconds sizing up the two men in front of him. Mark was just the same as he'd been the day before, except a little angrier and a little more cautious. The other man was doing his best to put on a tough facade, but was obviously there to follow Mark's lead. Both of them were armed.

"What's the matter?" Mark asked as he planted his feet and leaned forward. "You go deaf? I asked you a question. Where's Lynn?"

"If she wanted to see you, she'd be with you," Clint replied.

"Don't bother with what I got going with her. You just tell me where she's at and you won't get hurt."

Clint stood his ground without moving a muscle. His eyes darted back and forth between Mark and the other man as a cold wind blew past them.

"Who'd you bring with you?" Clint asked. "Backup?"

Mark gritted his teeth and snapped, "I don't need anyone to back me up. If you don't answer my damn question, I'll drop you right here and then go find Lynn myself."

"I don't think you could find your own hat if it was nailed to your head. Now, why don't you go find yourself another woman who'll put up with the likes of you? Something tells me Lynn's more than you can handle."

"You think so, huh?"

"I know so," Clint replied. "Why don't you ask her yourself? Oh, that's right. She ran from you like you had the plague, didn't she?"

Hearing that, the man next to Mark let out a chuckle. He quickly tried to choke it back, but wasn't quick enough to do so before Mark turned to glare at him.

"You think that's funny, Joey?" Mark grunted.

Joey shook his head. "No, I just—"

"Then shut yer damn hole and help me bury this cock-sucker."

When Joey shifted his eyes toward Clint, he found Clint already staring at him with a deadly fire burning in his eyes. Joey didn't want to hold Clint's gaze and quickly looked back at Mark. "Lynn's probably back at the hotel by now. Why don't we look for her there?"

"What?"

Still keeping his eyes away from Clint, Joey added, "That bitch is more trouble than she's worth. You said so, yourself."

Mark pulled the gun from his holster and spoke in a voice that sounded as if it had been dried out and torn to shreds. "I can say whatever I please about her. She's mine, you hear? Mine!"

Clint would have been content to let Mark spout off all he wanted. He drew the line, however, when he saw the gun leave Mark's holster. Seeing that, Clint reacted out of pure reflex and drew his modified Colt in a one fluid motion.

A single shot barked from the Colt and clipped a piece from Mark's sleeve. Mark pulled his arm away with a surprised expression that was almost funny. As soon as he saw Clint standing there with a smoking pistol in his hand, Mark let out a profane grunt and shifted his aim in Clint's direction.

The modified Colt spat out another round and bucked against Clint's palm. This time, the bullet sparked against Mark's gun. It was pure luck that the round ricocheted from there and whipped past Joey's head.

Mark couldn't toss his gun away fast enough. His face had turned beet red from his own anger, and he was fit to be tied when he saw Joey back away from him and Clint.

"Son of a bitch!" Mark hollered.

Clint kept his pistol aimed at Mark and said, "Next time

I see you, I'll figure you're out to shoot me. Whatever happens after that will be self-defense."

"She's mine, goddammit," Mark shouted. "I'll take her back whether you like it or not. I'll have her back whether *she* likes it or not!"

"Just leave."

Without a gun in his hand or any friends to back his play, Mark didn't have many options other than the one Clint had given him. "She's a whore, you hear me?" Mark said as he backed away. "You can have her."

Clint stood his ground and watched as Mark sputtered and kept shuffling backward toward the town. He didn't pay any mind to the obscenities rolling from Mark's mouth or the gestures he made with his wildly flailing hands.

Once Mark turned tail and ran, Clint holstered his Colt and started walking back to the hotel. He kept his eyes open for either of the two men to come at him again, but there was no trace of Mark or Joey. Clint's mind shifted to more pleasant thoughts when he caught a whiff of bacon coming from one of the nearby restaurants.

SEVEN

"I'm glad Mark didn't hurt you," Lynn said as she pulled apart one of the fresh biscuits that had been set onto her plate.

Clint picked up a strip of bacon and snapped off an end that was burned just right. "You heard about that, huh?"

"It's a small town, Clint. All I needed to do was open a window to hear it." She shrugged and showed him a tired smile. "Sorry about that. I feel like maybe I am more trouble than I'm worth."

"I won't hear any talk like that. Seems like all you did wrong was spend too much time with an asshole like Mark. Stepping in was my choice and coming after me today was his."

"All right then," Lynn said with a wider smile. "At least let me pay for breakfast."

Shaking his head slowly, Clint said, "I don't know if you'll want to do that. I haven't even gotten started yet."

"I think you've earned a big breakfast." With a subtle wink, she added, "You earned it after our third go-around last night."

Clint couldn't exactly argue that point, so he picked up

his fork and tore into the stack of griddle cakes in front of him. He didn't stop until he was halfway through the delicious cakes. After drinking some coffee to wash them down, he asked, "So what did you ever see in a man like Mark anyhow?"

That caused the cheery smile to drop right off Lynn's face. "Let's not talk about him anymore, Clint."

"Just making conversation."

She sighed and bought a few seconds by taking some bites of her own breakfast. When she saw Clint still looking at her, she gave in. "He came along and said some sweet things at the right time. To be honest, we only met up a few times over the last year. He'd come and go while I went about my own business.

"I thought we were just meeting up when we could and going our separate ways when we couldn't. It turns out, he thought we were together for a year and two steps away from the altar."

Clint laughed and took another bite. "Good Lord."

"How do you think I felt? I wanted to visit a friend of mine and he said he'd come along as far as . . . well . . . here. He caught wind of me spending a bit of time with someone else and lost his mind."

"That's it?" Clint asked.

"Isn't that enough?"

"I mean, that's all that led up to this whole mess?"

She thought about it for a few seconds, but couldn't think of anything else to add. So Lynn simply nodded and said, "Yep. That's it."

Shaking his head, Clint could only say the words he had already said. "Good Lord."

As she looked back on it, Lynn had to laugh as well. It wasn't much of a laugh, but more of a tired couple of breaths that shook as she let them out.

"So what did Mark do while he was away?" Clint asked.

Lynn paused with a fork halfway up to her mouth and shrugged. "I think he worked on a few trail drives or maybe did some scouting."

"You think?"

"I honestly don't even know for sure. Most of the times, I was hoping he would just go away and not come back. This time was different. There were some other men who came around as if they were up to no good, and Mark chased them away."

Clint narrowed his eyes and asked, "Really?"

She nodded. "That's why I agreed for him to come along with me this far. Truth be told, I was going to part ways with him before I left. I figured it'd be best if I did it then when I was planning on leaving anyway."

"Leaving where?"

"Dodge City. I worked there as a faro dealer for a few different saloons. It was pretty good work for a while."

Chuckling as he took another sip of coffee, Clint said, "Good work for a cheat, from what I've seen."

"Or good work until they expect you to cheat."

"You refused to stack the odds for the house?"

Lynn waited for a few seconds, but couldn't keep the mischievous smile from her face. "Actually, I just wasn't very good at cheating. I knew the tricks, but I couldn't get a knack for pulling them off." She only had to watch Clint for a few more seconds before noticing the expression on his face. "And don't preach to me, Clint Adams. Every gambler cheats and most folks expect faro dealers to be running some sort of game."

"Just so long as they don't get caught."

"Yes," she replied. "And that's why I was given my notice from that saloon. Before I got through the door on my last day, every place in town knew about me. I thought I could serve drinks, but every faro player in town came asking me how a game was rigged or any number of things, so I left."

"And you came here?" Clint asked. "Must be awfully strange after living in a place like Dodge."

"I'm just passing through," she quickly told him. "I'm headed west to a town called Thickett."

"Actually, that sounds worse. Maybe you should stay here."

"I'm going to stay with an old friend of mine. Her father owns a farm out there and he's got some space for me to live until I can scrape together enough money to head farther west."

"California?"

Lynn brightened up as if Clint had correctly told her fortune. "How'd you know that?"

"Call it a hunch. You look like you'd be at home on the Gold Coast. Don't tell me you're working your way there by stage."

"Oh, no. I'll catch a train in Wichita and ride from there. I just need to save up for the ticket." Lowering her eyes and poking at her breakfast, Lynn added, "I also need to make it to Thickett in one piece. With Mark acting the way he is, I though . . ."

"What if I come along?" Clint asked before she could get around to it. It was worth the effort just to see the surprise on Lynn's face grow even brighter than it had been a few moments ago. "But there is a price."

"Name it."

"Tell me how to clean up in faro."

EIGHT

Although he didn't come right out and tell her, Clint wasn't about to let Lynn ride out of Spelling by herself. He also wasn't about to let her stay there, since Mark Rowlett would have been able to mess up both of those simple plans just by being there.

Lynn had intended on staying put until the next stage came through town, but Clint decided to offer the back of his saddle as a way to speed up the process of getting her on her way. She was more than happy to climb onto Eclipse's back and wrap her arms around Clint as they put the small town behind them.

It would have been a couple days' ride to Thickett, but Clint knew a shorter route than the stagecoaches used. Eclipse was also a hell of a lot faster than any team of overworked horses pulling a wagon. The Darley Arabian stallion thundered down the narrow trail like the wind. He barely even seemed to feel the extra weight of Lynn sitting on his back.

Kansas may have been easy to ride through, but there wasn't a whole lot to look at. Clint thought he may have been spoiled after spending so much time in places like the

Badlands, the Rocky Mountains or even the deserts of New Mexico.

He kept his eyes open for any trace of Mark or anyone else who might decide to follow him. When he came up short on that end, he was forced to pay closer attention to the landscape itself. Tall grass swayed all around, keeping slow time to the gentle breeze. To some, the sight might have been relaxing. For Clint, it made it difficult for him to stay awake.

The air was dry.

The grass parted for Eclipse like a tall, feathery ocean.

It was easy to see just about anything at all for miles in every direction.

The terrain allowed Eclipse to run at a full gallop most of the time.

Still, Clint found himself wishing for a bluff to climb or even a river to cross. As soon as he spotted the glint of sunlight reflecting off water, he pointed Eclipse in that direction and held on. In no time at all, they'd arrived at a small lake and Clint was pulling Eclipse to a stop.

"What a perfect day to ride," Lynn said cheerily as she took the hand Clint offered to help her down.

"I suppose."

"At least there's nobody shooting at you," she offered.

"I think I'd welcome the change of pace."

When she stretched her back and took a few steps to stretch her legs, Lynn looked around and then looked back to Clint. "What's wrong with this?" she asked while holding out her arms. "It's a pretty day."

"Sure, but . . . I suppose I don't like rides where I could fall asleep in the saddle and not be any worse off."

She shrugged and replied, "I guess I don't think about that since I was born and raised in Kansas. It does me good to feel like I'm the only one on the face of the earth sometimes. After dealing with the likes of Mark Rowlett, I'd think you could understand that."

"I suppose," Clint said as he led Eclipse to the lake. "I'm just a little more accustomed to having other things to look at apart from grass."

"Like what? Sand? Rocks?"

Now that Eclipse was drinking, Clint could drop the reins and walk over to Lynn. She had her back to him with her arms crossed and her head tilted up into the breeze. Clint stepped up behind her and wrapped his arms around her waist.

"Like you, for one thing," Clint said. "I'd much rather look at you than a field of grass."

Lynn didn't open her eyes, but she did lean back against Clint and smile contentedly. "I guess I can't fault you for that."

The wind blew some of Lynn's hair against Clint's face, filling his nose with the sweet scent of her. Just as he was about to lean in and kiss her neck, Clint spotted something moving in the distance that wasn't just another patch of long, swaying grass.

When she felt Clint's arms leave her waist, Lynn snapped her eyes open and looked around. "What's the matter?" she asked when she saw Clint rushing toward Eclipse.

Clint didn't answer her right away. Instead, he took the spyglass from his saddlebag and put it to his eye. The other horses were a ways off, but they were still too close for Clint's liking.

"Looks like we're not the only ones out enjoying this fine day," he said.

NINE

There was no need to hurry away from the lake. If the men riding those horses were following him, Clint knew they would have already spotted him. Then again, if they were simply passing by, they would have moved on by now.

"Let me see," Lynn said as she held out a hand.

Clint passed the spyglass over to her and said, "Be my guest. See if you can recognize—"

"That's Mark," she said quickly.

"Are you sure? You barely even had a chance to get a look at them. Take a good look. From this distance, it could be easy to see a few things that aren't really there."

Lynn kept the spyglass to her eye and shook her head slightly. "I know it's him, Clint. Those patches of white on his horse make it look like it's wearing a fancy shirt. I used to tell him that all the time. See?"

Clint took the spyglass and looked through it again. Before too long, he had to admit, "I can't really tell too much. I can see some white on the horse, but that's about it."

"It's Mark's horse. And since he loves that horse more than anything else, it's got to be him in the saddle." She paced and wrung her hands. "He's following us."

"Probably."

Although she just stood there for the next couple of seconds, there was enough tension building up on Lynn's face to make her seem more like a teakettle that was about to start whistling. When she reached her boiling point, she stormed over to Eclipse and reached for the rifle hanging from the Darley Arabian's saddle.

"I'll finish this right here and now," she said. "After everything that man's put me through, I deserve to be the one to put him down like the dog he is."

Clint raced forward when he saw what she was trying to do and just managed to catch her hand before she could get the rifle in her grasp. "How about you give me a chance before you do anything too drastic?"

Lynn nodded. "Sure. You're probably a better shot than me."

"That's not exactly what I had in mind."

"Well, that's what you're going to have to do to shake him loose. Believe me. I've tried everything else."

Since Eclipse had had his fill, Clint took his reins and led him away from the water. "For right now," he said, "why don't you just try trusting me and see if I can do something to dissuade our mutual friend?"

Watching Clint sternly, Lynn let out a frustrated sigh when she saw him climb into the saddle and reach down to help her up. "Fine," she huffed. "But I get to take a shot at him if this doesn't work."

"It's a deal. Now, do me a favor and hang on."

With that, Clint snapped the reins and tapped his heels against Eclipse's sides. The Darley Arabian stallion responded as if he'd been waiting for that order all day long, and bolted away from the lake as if his tail was on fire.

It took Clint a few seconds to get settled and find Eclipse's rhythm. Once he and Lynn were situated and not about to be thrown from the saddle, Clint looked over his shoulder. At first, he didn't see a trace of the horses. Even so, he let Eclipse keep running for a while.

When he looked back again, Clint could see some dust swirling over a spot of the trail that hadn't been kicked up by Eclipse. Soon, he saw two horses break through the dust and fall into step a ways behind him.

"That's Mark, all right," Clint shouted over the thunder of Eclipse's hooves. "Either that, or it's someone else who wants to tag along with us."

Lynn tried to get a look behind her, but she wasn't able to twist around very far without endangering her own balance. Facing forward once more, she said, "I told you so. Now what?"

"Now you'll hang on just like I asked before."

Lynn didn't need to be asked twice, especially since Eclipse was already moving fast enough to make her nervous. She cinched her arms around Clint and pressed her head against his shoulder.

Hunkering down a bit, Clint gave his reins an extra flick and coaxed a bit more speed out of Eclipse. But it wasn't exactly speed that he was after. Instead, Clint wanted to allow the stallion to build up some momentum for what he had in mind next.

As soon as he spotted a fairly clear patch alongside the trail, Clint steered away from the beaten path. Eclipse did as he was told, leaving the smooth dirt trail for the rougher terrain alongside it. For the first few yards, there wasn't a huge difference. Before too long, however, it became clear as to why a trail was meant to be followed in favor of just riding anywhere the wind blew.

Animals had dug holes here and there, which made the ground a bit unsteady. There were fallen logs as well as a few rocks scattered about. The farther Clint got from the trail, the closer he had to watch the upcoming ground for potential hazards.

"You're right," Clint shouted over his shoulder. "This country isn't as dull as I'd thought."

But Lynn didn't seem to be as amused as Clint. In fact,

she didn't even try to respond to what he'd said. She simply kept her face down and her arms wrapped tightly around him.

Eclipse responded to the reins so well, it seemed as if the stallion knew what Clint was thinking. One subtle tug or flick here and there got the Darley Arabian to jump over a log or steer around the occasional hole. Although Lynn seemed to be breathing easier as the ride leveled out, Clint was hoping for a bit more to work with.

Looking over his shoulder, he spotted the two horses doing a fairly good job of keeping on his tail. Suddenly, Eclipse left the ground and sailed a yard or two through the air to land with a jarring thump on the other side of a large carcass that had been lying in the way. Clint turned around so he could pay better attention to what was in front of him rather than the two shapes behind.

From what he'd seen, Clint could tell the two riders were following pretty closely in his own path. That gave Clint an idea as to what he should look for. As luck would have it, he only had to ride another quarter of a mile or so before he found it.

Directly in front of Clint, a dirty rock lay slightly to the left and a thick tree stump with a splintered top sprung up to the right. Doing his best to alter his course without being too obvious, Clint pointed Eclipse toward the rock and snapped the reins.

The Darley Arabian was going so fast that the rock and the stump sped up on him within seconds. At the last moment, Clint gave the reins a little pull to the right and Eclipse veered slightly in that direction. They came so close to the rock that Clint was surprised he didn't feel it brush past his foot. The stump was a little farther off than he'd hoped, but he figured it would still do the trick.

Clint turned in his saddle to take another look behind him. Sure enough, the two who had been following were racing up at what had to be the fastest their horses could go. As Clint watched, they reached the rock and steered around it. One of them went left and the other went right. The one who went right had to think awfully quickly once he saw the stump threatening to send his horse to the dirt.

The rider pulled back on his reins hard enough to cause his horse to rear up and pump its front legs into the air. Clint grinned as he and the second rider left that one behind in a matter of seconds.

Spotting a group of trees, Clint steered toward them and hoped the remaining rider cared enough about his partner to hang back at least for a few seconds to see if the man was all right. Clint made it to the trees, which were just thick enough for Eclipse to stand behind.

"He'll catch us," Lynn whispered.

"Maybe," Clint replied. "Maybe not."

"At least get the rifle ready. If Mark follows us this far, I want to be the one to—"

But the rest of Lynn's threat was swallowed up by the rumble of hooves as they pounded against the ground less than fifteen yards away from them. Although the horse got fairly close, it kept moving and faded away before closing in on them completely.

When Lynn opened her eyes, she found Clint looking at her with a wide smile on his face. She looked back to the trail behind them, but couldn't see much through the trees. She looked to either side and saw nothing. When she looked ahead, she saw the dust that had been kicked up by the rider as he had raced past them.

"How'd you know he would do that?" she asked.

"I didn't."

"You what?"

Clint shrugged and asked, "Would you have believed me if I'd told you I knew what would happen?"

"No."

"Then take your good luck when you can get it," Clint said as he snapped his reins and got Eclipse moving away from the trees in a direction other than the one the rider had taken. "Any self-respecting faro cheat would know that much."

TEN

Despite the confidence Clint showed as he sat upright in the saddle and tossed a few boasts back toward Lynn, he was surprised that the two riders didn't show themselves for the rest of the day. He was even more surprised when he spent the entire next day without seeing so much as a hint of them.

Shaking the riders off his trail had been a fun diversion from a boring ride. His blood was racing for the rest of the day, which had turned to an uncomfortable anxiousness soon after. When they made camp, Clint took extra care to find spots that wouldn't be easily attacked. He stayed up as long as he could to keep watch and slept with one eye open just in case the riders decided to pay him a visit.

But they didn't get any visitors.

As they closed in on the neatly arranged streets and storefronts that were Thickett, Lynn began to act as if some of Clint's confidence had finally rubbed off on her. Rather than hang onto him for dear life, she kept her arms wrapped around him as if she was simply doing so because she wanted to.

"Another nice day," she said.

"Don't say that."

"Why?"

"Because," Clint replied, "things haven't turned out so well when you've talked like that."

"Things have worked out just fine," Lynn told him. "We're here and it took less time than I thought it would."

"That's because we rode like bats out of hell for most of the way."

Clint felt a little slap against his shoulder before Lynn let out a laugh.

"You can gripe all you want," she said. "You're not going to convince me things are anything but perfect."

"Perfect may be pushing it a bit," Clint said. "But I will admit the ride had its good spots."

"You mean like last night in camp?" she whispered.

"Yeah. That's exactly what I mean."

Thinking along those lines was enough to put a smile on Clint's face. Now that he was riding down Thickett's main street, he figured it was about time he allowed himself to let out the breath he'd been holding since he first realized he was being followed. For all he knew, Mark and the other rider had been scared off after being spotted and had given up on trying to catch up to them. Even if that wasn't the case, Clint knew it didn't do anyone any good to fuss about what other folks had in mind.

The town Clint saw didn't come close to living up to its name. Considering its name was Thickett, Clint couldn't think of a better compliment he could pay to the place.

Thickett was made up of a handful of streets arranged at nearly perfect angles. The boardwalks were straight and level, forming something close to a frame around well-maintained storefronts. Each shop was marked by a freshly painted sign and had some kind of decoration in every window. Even the sheriff's office was tucked away on a corner so as not to smudge the pretty landscape.

It was late afternoon when they arrived, so there was a fair amount of activity on the streets. In fact, Clint was surprised at how busy the place was considering its modest size. It was also a bit of a surprise since he had yet to see a saloon or gambling hall.

"Maybe you should live right here," Clint said. "I haven't seen a town this inviting for a while."

"I was just thinking the same thing. I wonder where someone would go to get a drink."

Clint chuckled and turned around to say, "That's good to hear. I figured I might get in trouble by asking that question."

Lynn winced and looked at the quiet folks watching them ride down the street. "You just might, at that."

"So do you want to get a drink?" Clint asked. "I'm sure there's a saloon around here somewhere."

"No. I'd rather look in on Tina."

"Tina?"

"She's my friend who lives here," Lynn said impatiently. "The reason why we came."

"That's right. Her father's the farmer, right?"

Patting him on the back, Lynn said, "That's right. Now you remember. I'm amazed you get anywhere other than lost with a memory like that."

Clint tipped his hat to a short row of men in battered overalls sitting outside of a bakery. "My memory's just fine. It's just that planning things too far in advance doesn't do me any good. Someone or something always crops up to spoil whatever I had in store for myself."

Lynn pulled in a sharp breath. "Is that what I've done? Oh, Clint, I didn't mean to—"

"Relax," Clint interrupted before she could get too upset. "I learned to be flexible way before I met you. And if I didn't want to help, I wouldn't have offered."

"All right, then. I won't bring it up again." And, just as suddenly as she'd pulled in that breath, Lynn was on to something else. "Wes's place is west of here. Or maybe northwest."

Clint pulled back on the reins to bring Eclipse to a stop while Lynn thought things over.

"Definitely west," she muttered. "Yes. That's it."

"How far west?" Clint asked.

When he didn't get an answer right away, Clint asked, "You're sure this is a good friend of yours?"

"She's a very good friend. I've just never been here before." Sliding down from the saddle, she said, "I'll get us some water and I'm sure it'll come to me."

Clint watched her hop onto the boardwalk and approach the men lined up in front of the bakery. Even from his spot in the street, Clint could hear Lynn talk to the men in the overalls.

"Do any of you fellows know where the Petrowski farm is?"

ELEVEN

Wes Petrowski was crawling in a pumpkin patch when Clint and Lynn rode up the road leading to his farm. The spread was actually due south of Thickett and was marked by a tall weather vane that squeaked loudly in the breeze.

At the first sound of Eclipse's hooves, Wes stuck his head up like a giant rabbit that had been caught eating a head of lettuce. He looked to be somewhere in his fifties, but could have been a decade older than that.

Like most farmers, Wes had been toughened up by the elements after spending years working in the middle of them. He wore a blue checkerboard shirt under a thread-bare denim jacket. His scalp and neck had a red hue to it, which made the ring of white hair around the back of his head stand out even more. Sharp eyes glared from beneath a furrowed brow. When he stood up, Wes was brandishing a hoe like it was a two-handed weapon.

"Who're you?" Wes asked. Although the man's voice wasn't exactly threatening, the look in his eyes showed he wasn't to be taken lightly by a couple of strangers.

If Lynn took notice of the old man's eyes or the hoe in his hand, she didn't show it. In fact, she jumped down from

Eclipse's back and ran up to him as if Wes was waiting for her with open arms.

"It's so good to see you!" she shouted. "I've heard so much about you!"

Wes didn't swing the hoe, but he didn't drop it either. He stood there like one of his own scarecrows, only with a more confused look on his face. Since Eclipse was facing the direction that gave Wes a clear look at Clint's holster, the old man kept his eyes pointed in that direction.

"I'm Lynn McKay," she finally announced.

That caused Wes to change his expression as drastically as night suddenly changing to day. "You're Lynn?" he asked as he shifted the hoe to one hand and wrapped his free arm around her. "What took you so long to get here?"

"There was some trouble along the way."

"If there's anything you need . . ."

Lynn chuckled at the protective tone in Wes's voice. "I'm fine. I have Clint, here, to thank for that."

Keeping one arm draped around Lynn, Wes stepped forward to extend a hand up to Clint. "Any friend of my daughter's is a friend of mine. The name's Wes Petrowski."

"Clint Adams," he replied while shaking Wes's hand.

The years of working the land shone through in Wes's grip. He shook Clint's hand as if he was kicking around the idea of breaking a few bones. Unlike most powerful handshakes, this one didn't seem to have any bad intentions behind it. The hand that was doing the shaking just happened to be strong as an ox.

"I hope you didn't pay for a room in town," Wes said. "I wouldn't have you sleep anywhere but under my roof."

"I wouldn't want to impose."

"Nonsense. You'll stay here and you'll have supper at my table. Tina would skin me alive if she found out I let it happen any other way."

Clint couldn't help but smile at the farmer's rough yet amicable nature. Rather than rile the old man, Clint tipped his hat. "Much obliged. Is there a place for me to put up my horse?"

"This is a damn farm, ain't it?" Suddenly, Wes winced as if he'd been smacked on the back of his head. "Pardon the language," he said to Lynn. "I've got more than enough space for you and your horse, Clint. Come on with me and I'll take you to the stable."

Since everyone else was on foot, Clint swung down from Eclipse's back and led the Darley Arabian by the reins. Wes and Lynn were already several paces ahead and chattering back and forth about what had brought her all the way across Kansas. Clint looked ahead a ways and spotted a few buildings at the end of a set of ruts. It looked to be a fairly good walk, but he was in no hurry to get there. In fact, it was relaxing to just take his time and mosey for once.

Clint rarely ever got the chance to mosey.

It didn't take long before he got to like it.

Now, if only the rest of the world would forget about him for a while and let him sit still for a change.

TWELVE

"I swear to God I'm gonna kill that son of a bitch," Joey muttered as he winced and got to his feet.

Lying stretched out in front of him was the horse that he'd just grown to like over the last few days. Now that horse was on its side and grunting in pain after tripping over a stump while chasing Clint.

"Are you ready to go or not?" Mark grunted. "That horse is done for."

"No, it ain't! Don't say that!"

Mark rode over to look down at the animal. Its eyes were glazed over, and the pain was clear enough to see on its face. Letting out a breath, Mark drew his pistol and put the wounded animal out of its misery.

"There," Mark said. "Now you can stop bellyaching about it."

"Dammit," Joey snarled. "I just stole that horse a week ago."

"Then you can steal another one and we can catch up to Lynn."

When he saw the fire in Joey's eyes, Mark tightened his grip on his pistol and aimed it in his direction. "You wanna start something with me or do you wanna take it up with the one who tripped up yer horse?"

The fire in Joey's eyes dimmed just a bit as he glanced back at the last spot in which he'd seen Eclipse.

"That's right," Mark said, latching onto the small opening he'd created. "He was hoping to trip us up and got you."

"We wouldn't even be out here if you weren't still stuck on that blonde," Joey grumbled.

Seeing that the danger had passed, Mark lowered his gun and dropped it back into its holster. "It won't take long to collect her. She'll either come back with me or I'll see to it she don't keep another man's company."

"And after that?"

"After that, we'll keep on with our own business. There's plenty to be done in these parts, and most of the lawmen don't even know us around here. Leastways, they won't as long as we stay away from Wichita."

"That's where all this trouble started," Joey pointed out.

"And here's where it'll end."

"Sure. If you know where to look to find her again."

Mark grinned. "I already know where to look. She's headed to a farm owned by a friend of hers. From there, she'll be movin' on to California. That's all she ever used to talk about."

"Where in California?" Joey asked. "That's a big stretch of land, you know."

"I don't know where, exactly. She talked about a few different places like San Francisco or Sacramento. That's why we need to catch up with her before she gets that far. And since I know where she'll be, that won't be a problem."

Although Joey looked optimistic at first, that quickly faded. "What about the fella she was with? He coulda killed us both."

"But he didn't. Not even close." Mark spoke with plenty of steam behind his words, but wasn't able to keep it up for long. In fact, by the time he took his next breath, that steam had evaporated. "We'll have to keep an eye on him, that's for certain. But he must not be a real killer; otherwise, we'd be dead."

"Yeah," Joey said meekly. "I suppose that's true enough."

"And if I know Lynn, she's got the man wrapped around her little finger. That's what she does."

Joey nodded. "Sure as hell. I saw what she did to you."

"Right. Now all we need to do is get to that farm, find them two and then wait for a spot to make our move."

"What move are you gonna make?" Joey asked.

Mark seemed to be looking at something far away. He didn't even seem to hear the question for a few seconds. Finally, Joey's words made it through to him and he shook his head slowly. "Don't worry about what I'm gonna do. You just worry about backing me up."

Just when Joey was about to throw himself behind Mark's plan, he stopped and cocked his head to one side like a dog that had just heard a strange whistle. "Wait a second. What's in this for me?"

That snapped Mark out of his faraway trance real quickly. "What do you mean by that?" he snapped.

"Just what I said. That fellow almost gunned us both down with some damn fancy shooting. If he wanted us dead, we'd both be in hell right now. I went along with you because we've seen some times together, but I don't wanna get killed just because you can't shake yourself free of this damn woman."

As soon as those words were out of Joey's mouth, Mark was lunging forward to grab hold of him by the throat. One hand was clamped around Joey's collar, while the other hand dug straight into Joey's windpipe.

"I won't hear you speak badly about Lynn, you hear?" Mark growled.

Even though his face was turning red and it was hard for

him to get a word out, Joey wheezed, "You said she was . . . no good. She ain't . . . worth dyin' over."

"That's my goddamn business," Mark said as he leaned in and tightened his grip. Suddenly, the viciousness in his eyes dimmed and some of the sense returned. Mark loosened his grip on Joey's throat, but kept hold of his collar. "That farmer does a good business. He's got money stashed."

"How do you know all that?"

"Because Lynn talked about him and how well he took care of his daughter. I don't know how much he's got squirreled away, but there's something. So long as I get Lynn, you can have whatever else there is."

Joey's eyes narrowed as he asked, "You swear?"

Mark nodded.

"Whatever money we find is mine? And you're sure there's money?"

"That's what I said, ain't it?" Mark announced. "Even if it's a hundred dollars, it's more than you got right now. All we need to do is bushwhack the man who's with Lynn and the rest is easy pickings." Putting an edge to his voice, Mark added, "You wanna make your living as a bad man, this is a good start. You wanna crawl away just because some asshole took a shot at you, then maybe you should be a damn farmer yourself. Or maybe you could just throw on a skirt and do some cooking?"

Using both hands, Joey pushed Mark back. "I ain't afraid of no man who don't have the sand to finish a fight. Where's this goddamn farm?"

THIRTEEN

If Clint had been looking for some peace and quiet, he certainly found it on the Petrowski farm. There was just something different about being on that much property owned and maintained by a man who cared about it. The rest of the world might seem wild, untamed and harsh, but the acres surrounded by such a meticulously tended fence were anything but.

Every patch of dirt had been turned over.

Every tree was in a row.

Not one weed could be seen.

Even the buildings in middle all looked as if they'd been painted on a canvas rather than pieced together using hammer and nails. As he followed Wes and Lynn around the place, Clint took in the sights and pulled in the air.

It was more than enough to bring a contented smile to his face.

"You can put that horse right in there," Wes said as he pointed to a building that was about half the size of the barn. "Take whatever stall you like and help yourself to anything else you need."

For a moment, Clint had forgotten he was leading Eclipse. The reins simply hung from his fist, and the Darley

Arabian followed behind as if he'd been lulled into the same contented daze as Clint. Shaking himself awake, Clint nodded and turned toward the stable.

"So where's Tina?" Lynn asked anxiously. "I thought I would've seen her by now."

"She should be back in an hour or so," Wes replied. "She went into town to get a new dress and Lord only knows what else. Once she gets to the store, she just loses track of everything else."

Lynn laughed and said something, but Clint couldn't make out what it was. He'd reached the stable by now, and even though the main doors were open, the sturdy wooden structure was built well enough to keep out most sound as well as the wind.

There were a few horses and a pair of mules in there, which left five empty stalls. All Clint needed to do was walk down the middle of the stable and wait for Eclipse to drift toward one stall. The stallion wasn't about to break free, but he did look toward one stall instead of any of the others.

"Not too often you get your pick like that, huh, boy?" Clint said as he took Eclipse into the stall and began un-hitching the saddle. "Looks like you'll be eating well for a while. Don't get too used to it. I don't have much use for a fat horse."

Eclipse settled in right away and started drinking from the trough before even looking at the hay beside it. After closing the stall's gate, Clint took a slow walk around to get a look at the rest of the animals in there.

All the horses were well cared for and strong. Even the mules seemed to be from fine stock, but that was surely because they saw plenty of work. By the time he got back to the main doors, Clint had a better idea of what Wes Petrowski was like as a person. A lot could be learned about a man by seeing how he treated his horses. So far, Wes seemed just as hospitable as he looked.

Clint took a few steps outside and found Wes and Lynn leaning against a hitching post and talking. While he didn't have anything against some leisurely conversation, Clint was enjoying his relaxing walk. Soon, he found himself wandering toward the barn and taking a look inside.

The barn looked like most others, although it was as well kept as the rest of the place. Clint had to smirk at the meticulous way every tool was in its spot and gleaming, as if every pitchfork's tong and every ax blade had just been polished. If not for all the care that had been shown to every little thing in there, Clint might have overlooked the messy pile of rags in the back corner.

Walking with his hands in his pockets, Clint made his way to the rags like a hound dog following an intriguing scent. As he stepped up to the pile, Clint looked around the wall above it for any lanterns or hooks where a lantern might hang. The last thing he wanted to think about was a good man like Wes losing a fine barn like this due to a careless fire being set.

There were no hooks and no lanterns close enough to be a worry. That much, at least, put Clint's mind to rest on the subject.

But Clint's mind wasn't at rest.

In fact, he couldn't get his eyes off those rags. Something about the way they were just piled up there so carelessly made them stick out like a sore thumb. Clint looked around at the rest of the barn just to satisfy his own curiosity. He wasn't about to go crawling around into every nook and cranny, but he could see more than enough to answer his question.

The rest of the barn was, indeed, as tidy as he'd first thought. Clint couldn't find one thing out of place apart from a few pieces of straw blowing across the floor or a small spot of chipped wood in one corner. Because of that, Clint found himself drawn back to the pile of rags.

He shrugged and let out a breath. It seemed the rest of

him wasn't so quick to let its guard down. Too much time spent dodging bullets, he figured. It only seemed right that an hour on a quiet farm wouldn't be enough to loosen all those knots he'd gained from having to draw blood to save his own life.

Looking toward the door, Clint could hear Wes and Lynn laughing and talking some more. He decided to join them rather than spend another minute trying to figure out a pile of rags. He laughed once to himself and kicked the pile with his toe as if proving how silly his frayed instincts were.

And, with that single tap of his toe, Clint was shown just how sharp his instincts were.

The pile of rags wasn't exactly what it seemed. In fact, the rags weren't piled up at all. They were covering something. Clint's boot had moved a few of them just enough for him to get a look at what they covered.

"Good Lord," he whispered as his eyes caught the sparkle of gold under the rags.

He nudged the pile again to find underneath the rags a hunk of gold almost as big as his head. It was enough gold to steal the breath right out of him.

FOURTEEN

Wes and Lynn didn't even notice Clint as he walked out of the barn. They were so busy swapping stories that they seemed surprised when they finally caught sight of him.

"There you are," Lynn said. "Is Eclipse all settled in?"

Clint nodded and replied, "Yep. I just hope he doesn't get to liking it too much in there. He might get spoiled."

"A happy horse runs faster," Wes said. "Don't worry none about his feed, though. I don't have anything in there that'd do him any harm."

"I'm sure you don't," Clint said. "This is a fine place you have here."

"Thank you kindly."

Making sure to watch Wes carefully, Clint added, "I wandered over to get a look in your barn. Hope you don't mind."

Wes may have flinched a bit, but it wasn't anything too serious. The older man nodded and put on a shaky smile. "If you like what you saw, I've got plenty of work for you to do."

"I may just take you up on that," Clint replied.

Both Lynn and Wes looked at him with an equal amount of shock on their faces. "You would?" they both asked in unison.

Clint laughed at their reaction and shrugged. "I can think of plenty worse places to spend some time. Of course, I wouldn't want to impose or go where I'm not wanted."

Wes started walking toward the house. "You don't have to do any work around here. You're welcome to have something to eat and stay as long as you like." When he reached the top of the steps leading to the front porch of his house, he stopped and pointed down the road. "Here comes Tina."

Lynn spun around on the balls of her feet and pulled in a deep breath. When she saw who was driving the one-horse cart approaching the house, she let out her breath in an excited scream.

The woman driving the cart was startled at first, but quickly recognized who was screaming. Soon, she was adding to the din with an excited scream of her own and squirming as if she was about to jump down from her seat and race the horse to the house.

When Clint looked to see what Wes was doing, he saw the old man covering his ears and stepping into the house. There wasn't anything suspicious there. In fact, the more noise both women made, the more Clint couldn't blame the old man for trying to find some shelter.

"Come here and meet my friend, Clint!" Lynn said excitedly.

Before he could think of a good excuse to get into the house, Clint felt Lynn take hold of his hand and pull so hard that she nearly yanked his arm from its socket. Clint went along with her to meet the cart as it came to a stop in front of the house.

Even in her spot in the driver's seat, it was easy to tell that Tina was a good deal shorter than Lynn. Thick, black hair flowed well past her shoulders and framed a thin, petite face. A little, upturned nose complemented delicate features, which were made even prettier by the bright smile adorning her face at the moment.

Tina tossed the reins aside and jumped down from the

cart so she could give Lynn a hug. "It's so great to see you!" she shouted. "I thought you might not show up."

"I said I would, didn't I?" Lynn asked.

"Yes, but from what you told me about Mark . . . Let's just say I'm glad you made it here so soon." Suddenly, Tina's eyes snapped over to Clint and some color flushed into her cheeks. "Oh. Is that . . . ?"

"No," Lynn said as she waved toward him. "That's not Mark. That's Clint Adams."

Taking that as his cue, Clint leaned forward and stretched out a hand. "Pleased to meet you."

Not only did Tina take the hand Clint offered, but she held onto it and pulled herself closer to him. "Nice to meet you too, Clint."

Tina was a small woman in her early twenties, but she had plenty of curves to make up for what she lacked in height. The dress she wore was a simple striped pattern that was buttoned to a respectable level, but it didn't do a thing to dampen the effect she had upon Clint. Her large breasts excited him as she stepped forward to look straight up into his eyes. The smoothness of her skin was inviting as she lingered there as if willing him to do more than just introduce himself.

The moment was shattered when Lynn pulled Tina away and smiled at them both. "You should have seen what Clint did to Mark," she said. "It was better than I would have imagined."

"And I know you imagined it a lot," Tina said. "I sure know I did, and I never even met him."

When Tina spun around to giggle with Lynn, Clint felt like he was in the middle of a windstorm. He could only stand there and wait for them to rush away toward the house.

Once they were gone, Clint was left by himself amid the combined scents of both women. He pulled in a breath and was reminded of both Lynn's hair and Tina's creamy shoulders. He had to shake his head to rattle himself back to the present, and when he looked at the house, he found Wes coming out of it.

"Kind of overwhelms you, don't it?" Wes asked.

Clint did his best to keep his thoughts about Wes's daughter from showing on his face. "Yeah. It sure does."

"They've always been like that when they got together. They were terrors when they were little girls and they're just as rambunctious now."

Chuckling under his breath, Clint shrugged and admitted, "That's not exactly how I would have put it, but you're right."

Wes stopped before climbing down the last step that led from his porch. His eyes were focused on Clint, and his mouth had turned into a hard, straight line. Clint could imagine what was going through the farmer's head, and he waited for the old man to give those thoughts a voice.

When he finally did speak, Wes's voice was every bit as sharp as Clint had expected.

"You haven't hurt that girl, have you?" Wes asked.

That had not been what Clint was expecting. He blinked and recalled the man's question a few times to make sure he'd heard it right. Finally, Clint asked, "You think I hurt your daughter?"

"Not her," Wes said coldly. "Lynn. I known that girl since she was knee-high to a grasshopper and she's always been sweet as pie. Maybe a little high-strung sometimes, but she's a good girl. Problem is, she don't know how to pick a good man. Tina's told me about some of the things Lynn told her and it made me sick. Are you one of those men that hurt Lynn?"

Clint could tell by the intent look in Wes's eyes that the farmer was watching Clint for any possible hint of a lie. Compared to the old man's scrutiny, most poker tables would have seemed downright hospitable.

"No," Clint said easily and clearly. "I've never hurt Lynn and I don't intend on doing anything of the sort."

After a few more seconds, Wes nodded. "All right, then. No hard feelings, I hope. I consider both of them girls my kin. They can be wild, but that don't mean they don't deserve someone lookin' out for 'em."

"I agree."

The smile that came onto Wes's face was as genuine as it was crooked. "Then come on inside. There's plenty of food to be served. I also got some home-brewed whiskey that'll curl your toes."

Clint followed Wes inside. He kept his own questions to himself for the time being. There was no need to spoil what promised to be a very interesting supper.

FIFTEEN

It was already dark by the time supper was ready to be served. At that time of year, the sun seemed to drop below the horizon like it was weighted down, as if it was doing its part to bring along another patch of cold. The moon was a sliver in the sky, giving the wind even more of a bite than normal.

Two shadows moved around more than the rest. They drifted from one spot to another, drawing closer to the farmhouse with every second. The wind howled just enough to cover the sound of the shadows' movements. But the brisk wind made the shadows stand out because they stayed still while all the grass and trees around them swayed slowly back and forth.

"I'm about to freeze to death," Joey grunted.

Mark kept his shoulder pressed against an old tree and his eyes on the brightly lit windows of the farmhouse's lower floor. "If you're gonna die, just do it quietly."

Gritting his teeth, Joey kept the rest of his complaints to himself. "Where the hell are they?" he asked.

"Where the hell do you think they are? A blind man could see they're in the house."

"I know that, but where? Do you think they saw us out here?"

"Not a chance," Mark replied with a quick shake of his head. "It's so dark out here, I can barely see my own boots. They're probably still eating. I can smell something cooking."

Joey pulled in a deep breath and held it as long as he could. "I can smell it too. Damn, I'm hungry."

"Then why don't you just walk up there and ask for a plate? Whether you get it or the farmer shoots you dead, at least I won't have to listen to your bellyaching."

"Fine, fine." Stepping around to the other side of the tree, Joey gazed at the house as if he could see the food on every plate. "Is Lynn and that other fellow here yet?"

"They got a big head start on us, didn't they?"

"Sure, but they could have stopped off somewhere else. Maybe their horse threw a shoe or . . . Hell, I don't know." Joey cupped his hands over his mouth, blew into them and then rubbed them together. "You're probably right. They did get a big head start."

But Mark didn't look happy to hear Joey agree with him. In fact, judging by the expression on his face, he seemed sick about it. Finally, he let out a groan and said, "Dammit. We should check just to make certain they're here."

"You want me to sneak up to a window?"

"No. They might see you." Mark squinted to try and hurry up the process of getting his eyes adjusted to the dark. Finally, he settled upon the pair of large buildings not far from the house. "One of those has gotta be a stable. If they're here, that fella's horse should be in there."

"You recall what it looked like?"

"Sure," Mark grunted. "Black with a white patch on the nose. Since you can't even remember that much, stay put and keep watch on the house. Anyone comes out, you let me know."

"How should I do that?"

"Make a noise. Throw a rock. Just catch my attention, for Christ's sake." The longer he spoke to Joey, the madder Mark got. It seemed that sharing a horse for the rest of the ride to the farm had taken a bigger toll than he'd expected. When he walked away from the tree, Mark was glad to get Joey out of his sight.

The wind was blowing past the house and toward the barn, so it carried even more of the smells from the dinner table to Mark as he walked along the path. The scents of home cooking made him reflexively relax as he approached the barn. By the time he got close enough to reach out for the door, Mark was able to pick out slightly more than shapes in the darkness. His eyes were adjusting to the night, but it was his ears that gave him something to use.

Another door slammed from not too far away, and footsteps were crunching against the narrow wooden step leading down from the side of the house. Mark crouched down and slapped his hand against his holstered pistol. He couldn't quite make out who was leaving the house, but he could see a person heading straight toward the barn.

SIXTEEN

Supper went off without a hitch. Tina and Lynn never stopped talking long enough for Clint or Wes to get a word in edgewise, and that was just fine. Wes was such a good cook that Clint wouldn't have had much to say anyway, since he had his mouth full most of the time.

Still, the gold Clint had spotted in Wes's barn sat in the back of his mind. Clint knew it wasn't any of his business if there was a river of gold running under the property, but he had to admit it was awfully peculiar.

Any man who'd found that much gold would do more than just dump it in a barn and cover it up with some rags. Judging by the condition the rest of the farm was in, there was no way for Clint to believe that Wes didn't know the gold was there.

As much as Clint wanted to just forget about it, he simply couldn't. Something didn't sit right with him. Unfortunately, those sorts of instincts rarely pointed Clint toward anything but trouble. If there was a way to snuff that instinct out, he knew he would have a much quieter life.

Then again, he thought, how much fun would that be?

Clint had been thinking a lot during the course of the meal. Once or twice, he'd even considered talking to himself since nobody else was speaking to him. That wasn't because of any rudeness on anyone's behalf. The girls were still chatting, and Wes was too busy straightening up the dishes to be bothered.

"I think I'll go out to stretch my legs," Clint said.

He got up from his chair and waited to see if anyone had heard him.

Apparently, they hadn't.

"Wes," Clint said while tapping the old man on the shoulder.

The farmer looked up at him and fixed his eyes intently upon Clint.

"I'm going to get some fresh air," Clint told him.

"Too stuffy in here for you?"

"No," Clint replied while patting his stomach. "Just need to walk some of this off."

Wes nodded and got back to what he was doing. "If anyone asks for you, I'll tell them where you went. I've known these girls for a while, so I wouldn't hold my breath on them coming up for air just yet."

"Thanks for the warning. I won't be long, though."

Rolling up his sleeves, Wes gathered up the last of the dishes and sunk his hands into a tub so he could start cleaning them off. Soon, the sound of plates clanking against each other was added to the chatter that had become constant between Tina and Lynn. Clint could tell it would take some work to break through all that commotion, so he simply walked past Wes and stepped out through the kitchen door.

Outside, the night was cold and dark. The longer he stood on the step that led down to the dirt trail joining all the buildings in the vicinity, the better Clint was able to pick out more than just shadows. As he walked toward the stable, his eyes had adjusted enough for him to spot the handle on the door.

Before he pulled the door open, Clint stopped and turned

to look toward the barn. He swore there was some movement in that area and squinted to try and pick out what had caught his attention. After a few seconds, he couldn't spot anything worth investigating so he went into the stable.

Eclipse was sleeping in his stall and barely stirred when Clint walked up to him. The Darley Arabian let out another deep breath and drifted back off.

After tossing a few handfuls of oats into the stall's feed trough and refilling the water, Clint stepped to the door and leaned against the frame so he could take a slow look around. There was plenty of movement around him, but it was difficult to pick out what was caused by the wind and what could have been something alive and kicking in the night.

Mark thought he'd been spotted for sure when Clint walked to the stable. His hand had gone to the gun at his side, but that only seemed to draw Clint's attention for longer. Once he stayed still, Mark only had to hold his breath and wait for Clint to look away. He didn't take another breath until Clint was inside the stable.

Since he'd thought Clint was heading toward the barn at first, Mark felt as if he'd dodged a bullet. Once Clint stepped into the stable, that gave Mark the opportunity to get to a better spot before his luck ran out. Even though he'd managed to duck around a corner, he knew he wasn't out of the woods just yet.

Squinting toward the nearby trees, Mark had to stare for a few seconds before he spotted Joey. Since it had taken him that long to pick out Clint, he figured Joey couldn't have been spotted by someone who didn't already know he was there. Before Mark could feel too secure, however, he saw Joey start to wave and walk over to the barn.

Mark started to shout for Joey to stay put, but stopped just short of making a sound. Instead, he hissed through clenched teeth and fiercely waved Joey back.

The dumb smile on Joey's face was plain as day. He returned Mark's wave with another friendly one of his own and started to run faster toward the barn.

Still trying to keep quiet, Mark leaned forward and let out a noise that was part whisper and part growl. He also waved Joey off, but it was too late to keep from being spotted. In fact, it looked as if both of them had been flushed out.

"Who's out there?" Clint asked as he took a step forward.

Mark leaned back around the corner of the barn and focused on Clint. At least he didn't have to wonder if Clint and Lynn had made it to the farm yet. Then again, judging by the way Clint was reaching for his gun, Mark might just have had bigger things to worry about.

SEVENTEEN

Clint was just starting to let his guard down when he saw someone moving toward the barn. The figure was a ways off and closer to the house than to him. Even so, Clint could see enough to realize it didn't look like Wes. Since it wasn't wearing a dress, it sure didn't look like either of the women.

"Who's out there?" he asked.

Nobody answered, but the figure did turn to look at him. By now, Clint could make out a few more details. The man looked younger and vaguely familiar, but there were still too many shadows around him for Clint to be sure of much more than that.

Letting his hand drift toward the Colt holstered at his side, Clint stepped forward. "Come on over here where I can see you."

The figure froze in his tracks and started to back away. His head kept twitching back and forth between Clint and the farthest corner of the barn.

As Clint looked toward the barn as well, he spotted another figure from the corner of his eye. This one was a bit closer, so Clint could make out a few details. The moment he caught a glimpse of a gun in the figure's hand, Clint drew the Colt and pivoted toward the barn.

The figure close to the barn fired a quick shot and ducked back behind some cover.

The figure out in the open, the first one Clint had spotted, drew a gun and started firing. The shots blazed through the air in quick succession, but were too wild to hit much more than the barn and stable.

With every muzzle flash, Clint was able to get a better look at the man's face. It wasn't long before he'd seen enough to realize who the person was. Once he knew that, Clint also knew who the other man must be.

"You came all this way to stir up more trouble, Mark?" Clint shouted as he ducked into the stable and peeked around the door. "You keep pushing your luck and you'll wind up dead."

"You're the dead man!" Mark shouted as he leaned out and fired another couple of shots.

Those rounds punched through the door frame not far from Clint's head. Although no blood had been drawn, the bullets came close enough to force Clint to back into the stable a bit more.

"That's him!" Joey shouted as he fired the rest of his shots at the stable.

"I can see that, dammit!" came the reply from Mark.

Clint grinned and shook his head, wondering if those idiots would shoot themselves before they got a clear shot at him. Suddenly, he realized what had brought him outside in the first place and where Mark was at the moment.

"Damn," Clint hissed under his breath as he hunkered down low and took another look outside.

As soon as Clint got a look at Joey scampering toward the barn, he saw a flash of sparks coming from the house. The flash was followed by the unmistakable roar of a shotgun.

"Whoever you are, get the hell off my property!" Wes shouted from where he stood just outside the house.

Joey didn't know which way to run. Although he wanted to get to the barn, he'd almost been shot for that. He couldn't exactly run away from the barn, since that would bring him closer to the house. His horse must have been tied up behind the house as well, because he nearly tripped over himself to turn around that way.

Hoping to force Joey to make a decision before Wes reloaded, Clint aimed and sent a round at Joey's feet. The bullet punched into the ground within inches of Joey's boots, causing him to hop and start running like a noisy target in a shooting gallery.

As humorous as that sight may have been, Clint didn't have time to laugh before he was forced to do some scrambling of his own. A bullet from Mark's gun drilled into the stable door and sent splinters raining down on Clint's head. Rather than cower back like Mark surely wanted, Clint steeled himself and charged forward instead.

Mark's gun barked two more times, putting a few rounds closer than Clint had anticipated.

Hot lead hissed past Clint's ear, and another piece dug a fiery trench through the meat of his upper arm. Clint let out a curse and jumped back into the stable. When he landed and examined his wound, he was more upset at himself for being stupid than at Mark for firing the shot.

Before Mark could follow up with another pull of his trigger, Wes pulled his own trigger. The shotgun's roar blasted through the night and was followed by the crunch of buckshot shredding through wood.

The wound in Clint's left arm was messy, but nothing serious. After wiping away some of the blood that had seeped out, he could see a nasty gash through his flesh that looked more like it had been put there by a wild animal's claw. He pushed the pain to the back of his mind as he reloaded and hurried toward the back of the stable.

Sure enough, there was a rear door. Clint threw the latch up and pushed the door open just enough for him to get a look outside. Compared to the chaos out front, the scene in back of the stable was genuinely tranquil. Rather than wait for more hell to erupt, Clint kept his head down and ran outside.

When Clint was halfway to the back of the barn, he saw a smaller door swing open and Mark race outside. Although Clint had been hoping to sneak up on Mark, he supposed this was the next best thing.

As if sensing Clint was there, Mark turned on his heels and glanced toward the stable. He picked Clint out right away and brought his gun around to start firing. Mark's pistol spit out a tongue of sparks and smoke as it was fired again and again.

The shots were just quick enough to force Clint to the ground, but not accurate enough to keep him there. When he looked up from where he'd dropped, Clint had a clear shot at Mark.

Suddenly, a shotgun went off behind and to the right of Clint. The blast caused Clint to reflexively press himself against the ground. It also caused Mark to leap for the corner of the barn in a desperate attempt to get some cover.

Since he let out a pained yelp, it was obvious that some of the buckshot had found Mark. Since he was nowhere to be seen when Clint looked up again, it was obvious that he wasn't hurt badly enough to have been stopped. One of the women at the house let out a scream as horses rumbled toward the barn and then rumbled away.

Clint scrambled to his feet and was just in time to see both men on horseback and racing away from the farm. They fired a few shots over their shoulders, but that did as much good as one might expect from the proverbial shot in the dark.

"They're gettin' away!" Wes shouted as he closed the breech of his shotgun and brought the weapon to his shoulder.

Clint was about to try and stop the old man, but he wasn't quick enough to get a word in before Wes pulled his trigger. The shotgun blasted once more, but the horses were much too far away to have been in any danger.

Watching the old man for a few seconds, Clint noticed that Wes glanced nervously at the barn before checking up on the women one more time. At least that put Clint's mind to rest regarding the outside chance that Wes didn't know about the gold hidden under those rags.

EIGHTEEN

Tina rushed outside with Lynn not too far behind. Locking her eyes on her father, Tina yelled, "What happened, Daddy? Who were those men?"

"Get back inside," Wes shouted at her. As soon as the words came out, he seemed to be just as surprised by the ferociousness in his voice as the young women were. Forcing himself to ease up a bit, Wes added, "I think they're gone, but you two should stay safe until we're sure."

Tina nodded and started to walk back to the house. Although she grabbed Lynn's wrist to pull her along, Tina wasn't able to budge the tall blonde from her spot.

"That was Mark," Lynn said as she fixed her eyes on Clint. "I know it was."

"Yeah," Clint replied. "It was him and that other fellow who was with him when we crossed their paths before."

Lynn pulled her hand free of Tina's grasp and took a few steps as if she meant to follow Mark's horse. The horses were out of sight, but the sound of their hooves could still be heard as they raced away from the house. If she'd had a gun in her hand, there was no doubt in Clint's mind that Lynn would have fired at the sound of those horses.

"Were they after you, Lynn?" Tina asked.

Lynn nodded slowly. "Yes. He always said I couldn't get away from him. The only reason I stuck around so long was because I'd started believing that. But then . . ." Her eyes drifted toward Clint and she gave him a weary smile.

After a second or two, Lynn let her head droop and she walked toward the house. Tina rushed alongside her, asking question after question as they went.

That left Clint and Wes outside on their own.

For a little while, neither one of them knew what to say.

Clint waited until he caught Wes glancing toward the barn one more time.

"You think they found it?" Clint asked.

"Found what?"

Letting out a breath, Clint eased the Colt back into its holster and crossed his arms over his chest. He stood there until Wes finally lowered the shotgun.

"I, uh . . . went into the barn," Clint explained.

"Yeah?"

Clint nodded. "I went in there just to have a look around. It was when I first got here. Tell you the truth, I guess I was just poking around where I had no business going. I stumbled upon that . . . pile of rags."

Instead of the anger or panic that Clint had been expecting, Wes simply nodded again. "Of course you did," he muttered.

Not knowing whether or not it was safe to approach the farmer while he was still holding a shotgun, Clint took one step toward him just to test the waters. Wes didn't do anything in return.

"I honestly didn't mean any harm," Clint said. "Everything else was so neat, those rags just kind of stuck out. Fires get started from things like that, you know."

"I know."

"And all I did was tap them with my boot." Clint stopped and watched Wes closely. When he saw the farmer still keeping still and remaining calm, it was Clint's turn to be confused. "I thought you'd be angry."

"Actually, I'm glad you found it. I've only had that damn rock for a few days and it's already been a pain in my ass."

The confusion in Clint's gut swelled up so much that he nearly choked on it. "It seems like a rock like that would solve plenty of problems. That is . . . if it's what it looked like it was."

"Oh, it's genuine, all right," Wes said. Suddenly, he seemed awfully uncomfortable standing out there. Gripping his shotgun, he said, "Let's get inside. The girls will need to have their minds put to rest and I don't want to give those two assholes an easy target. It don't take brains to fire a rifle."

"It sure don't," Clint said. He followed the farmer back into the house. Even after all that had just happened, the neat little home was still comforting.

NINETEEN

Wes spent a little while assuring his daughter he was all right. Although Tina had seemed to be worked up before, she calmed down as soon as she saw her father wasn't just trying to make her feel better. She fussed with him for a few more minutes as Lynn set her sights on Clint.

"Come on," she said as she took him by the hand. "Let me get a look at that arm."

"It's nothing," Clint insisted. "Really."

"I won't hear any of it. Just let me take a look and see what I can do. If you don't come along of your own accord, I'll have to get rough."

The insistent smile on Lynn's face was hard enough to resist. The soft touch of her fingers upon his hand made Clint want to go wherever she was leading him. Since he'd wanted to hear what Wes had to say, Clint looked over to where the old man was seated.

The farmer was in an old chair in the sitting room, allowing his daughter to buzz around him like a bee. It was obvious that Tina wasn't through fussing over him and that Wes wasn't about to run off anytime soon once she was done. Just to drive the point home, Wes gave Clint a weary nod as if to tell him whatever he'd wanted to say could wait.

"Do you two have something planned?" Lynn asked.

"Not exactly."

"Because if you want to hunt down those two, you've got my blessing."

Clint was about to say that hunting them down probably wasn't going to be necessary. If they'd come back this time, they would more than likely try again later. But that wouldn't have made Lynn feel any better, so he kept it to himself.

Also, Lynn wasn't stupid. She had to know what Clint was thinking without him telling her.

"If I tried running off now," Clint said, "you'd just have to get rough and pull me back. Remember?"

"Yeah," she said. "I remember. Now let's get a look at that arm."

She'd taken him into a small bedroom that was decorated with a few pictures on the wall and a few doilies draped over the little round tables set up on either side of a bed. There wasn't enough for it to look like someone slept there regularly, so it was probably a guest room. As neat as the rest of the house was, this room had Tina's touch all over it.

Lynn's hands were soft and gentle on Clint as she guided him to a bed that was just the right size for one person. Blankets and quilts were piled there to make Clint's landing as soft as possible as he dropped down.

"Careful," she said. "You've been through enough as it is."

Clint watched as she slowly reached out to pull open his shirt and peel it away from his body. Her eyes wandered along his chest and shoulders before finally settling upon the wound on his arm. She didn't shy away from the sight and even traced her fingertips gently along the bloodied skin.

"Does that hurt?" she whispered.

He shook his head. "Not too bad."

Lynn smiled and reached for the washbasin nearby. Since there weren't any cloths on the table, she cupped her hand and dipped it into the water. Her movements were careful and deliberate as she took her handful of water from the basin to Clint's arm. Drops trickled along her arm before dripping off her elbow. Finally, she wiped the water onto him.

It was cold and sent a bit of pain through Clint's arm, but he only let out a slight wince.

"Did that hurt?" she asked.

Clint played it up as he replied, "Yeah. A bit."

"Aww. Let me just get it cleaned up and then I'll help you feel better."

Since Clint was sitting on the edge of the bed, Lynn straddled one of his legs as she reached back and forth between him and the basin. Every time she refilled her hand with water, she wriggled herself against his knee. And every time she put the water on him, she was sure to get some of it on herself.

The more she cleaned him off, the less the wound hurt. Partly because the water was cold enough to numb him a bit. And partly because he was becoming more and more distracted as Lynn kept working on him!

While taking a closer look at the wound, she scooted in toward him. Leaning forward, her hair brushed against the side of Clint's face like a curtain that separated them from everything else. Her slender, muscular leg was also just far enough along his thigh to brush between his legs in just the right way.

Smiling at the effect she was having on him, Lynn said, "I don't even think this needs stitches."

"You don't? And when did you become a doctor?"

"And when did you become such a baby?"

"A baby?" Clint asked. "That's a bullet wound, you know. I thought you were going to make me feel better."

She started to laugh, but slipped one hand behind his

head and pulled him forward as she leaned in to place her lips on his mouth. Her entire body slid up closer to him while her other hand drifted between his legs.

Her lips were soft and warm. Lynn's hands were eager, and she used them to work Clint up so well that he forgot he'd even been in a fight earlier that evening.

"Are you . . . uh . . . sure your friend won't want to check in on you?" Clint asked.

Lynn slid her hand farther down, until she could stroke Clint's erection through his jeans. Turning at the waist, she reached back and shut the door. "She'll know better than to barge in. Besides, I'm not about to wait one more second."

Clint cupped her tight breasts in his hands and felt Lynn's little nipples grow hard against his palms. "I know exactly how you feel," he said.

TWENTY

Mark rode like a madman until he was sure to be out of range of the guns that were behind him. Even then, he kept riding just to be safe. When he pulled back on the reins, he looked around for Joey. When he'd started racing away from the barn, Mark had had Joey in his sight. Now Joey was nowhere to be seen.

Fighting back the urge to yell out Joey's name, Mark snapped his reins and kept riding in the same direction.

Still nothing.

Just as he was about to write the man off and call it a night, Mark caught a glimpse of Joey's horse. He assumed it was Joey's horse. Any animal would have to be out of its mind to gallop so fast through such thick darkness.

Mark snapped his reins and tapped his heels against his horse's sides. Within moments, he was closing the distance between himself and the other horse ahead. The man in the saddle was Joey, all right. And Joey damn near took a shot at Mark out of pure, twitchy reflexes.

"Put the fucking gun down!" Mark shouted.

There was more than enough venom in his tone to get Joey to do as he was ordered even if he couldn't hear Mark's voice. The command traveled like a slap through the air, forcing Joey to take notice and snap out of whatever had been gripping him.

"Mark? Damn, I'm glad to see you."

"So glad you're gonna put a bullet in me?" Mark asked.

Joey blinked and then looked at the gun in his hand as if he didn't even know what it was doing there. He lowered the weapon and waited for Mark to approach. "Are we off that farmer's land yet?" he asked.

"I think so."

"He's got a legal right to shoot us on his own land," Joey said as if he was reciting it from a vague memory. "Ain't that the way it is?"

"I don't know, but that don't even matter. If the farmer wants to come after us, it'll be the last thing he does. He got lucky, is all."

"He almost shot me in half!"

"He blindsided us while we were about to shoot the other fella."

Although Joey may have calmed down a bit, he didn't seem to be convinced about what Mark was saying. He started to nod, but wound up shaking his head. "I don't even know how close we got to killing that fella. Maybe we should—"

"Maybe we should keep riding for a bit before we kick back and have a nice conversation," Mark interrupted.

And before Joey could say another word, Mark snapped his reins and rode farther along the trail leading into Thickett. Joey followed along and picked up his pace once he was in sight of the town.

They rode down the street with the most people walking on it and didn't have any trouble finding a saloon. Even though the saloon wasn't what either of them was used to, they ordered a drink and got it quickly enough. Once Mark and Joey had tossed back their first shot of whiskey, they slowed down enough to get a better look at their surroundings.

"You sure this is a saloon?" Joey asked.

"That's what it says in the window."

Double-checking his own statement, Mark looked at the front window. Sure enough, the letters painted on the window marked the place as a saloon. The inside was still a whole lot cleaner and quieter than any saloon either man had frequented.

"As long as the whiskey comes," Mark said as they got their second drinks, "I don't give a damn if this is a Chinese laundry."

Joey showed his agreement by lifting his glass and downing the whiskey. After the firewater had burned its way to his stomach, Joey let out a slow sigh. "That's better," he said.

"Those two sure got awfully close, didn't they?" Mark asked with a grin.

"They sure as hell did. All I got to say is that woman better have gold between her legs for us to go through all this trouble."

"What'd I tell you about talking about her that way?" Mark snarled.

Joey held up a hand and shrugged. "I'm just saying. You know I'll ride along with you on a job where there's some profit involved, but this ain't worth it. That fella can handle a gun plenty better than we can. He's got the look of a genuine killer."

As much as Mark wanted to refute that assessment, he couldn't do so with a straight face. The farmer had come at them just as Mark had expected, but the other one was something else. Even though Mark swore he'd hit Clint at least once, that didn't seem to make a difference. Not every man could stand in the middle of gunfire and catch some lead without getting rattled.

"I don't know for certain if he's a killer," Mark said. "But he does know how to handle himself in a fight."

"You're damn right he does. We're in over our heads

and it ain't worth putting our lives on the line for that woman. There's plenty more women out there, Mark. This one's just too much trouble and you know it."

Mark mulled over those words and wasn't about to argue. But there was something else in his head as well. That was obvious by the anxious look in Mark's eye. Finally, he just came out and spoke his mind.

"Maybe we should look for someone else who can help us," Mark said.

"I don't know anyone around here," Joey replied.

"I'm not talking about someone we know."

"You mean a hired gun? We don't have that kind of money, and no gunman would go after that blonde for free unless he wanted her for himself."

Mark's eyes narrowed and a wolfish grin slid onto his face. Leaning forward with both elbows against the edge of their table, he whispered, "What if I saw something else in that barn that might be worth our trouble?"

"What if that fella's a gunfighter?" Joey asked.

"Forget about him. He's probably licking his wounds right along with that damn farmer."

TWENTY-ONE

Clint's arm was wrapped in a shred of material that had been ripped from the tail of his own shirt. Although some blood had soaked through the makeshift bandage, Clint didn't seem to take much notice of it. He sat on the edge of the bed wearing nothing but the scrap of ripped shirt. Lynn sat on his lap, facing him and straddling him with her long legs wrapped around his waist.

Lynn's arms were wrapped around Clint as well, as she rubbed his back and sifted her fingers through his hair. All the while, she squirmed and wriggled on him. Every now and then, she let out a stifled little moan.

Her skirts were hiked up around her waist and held there by Clint as he cupped her buttocks in both hands. They'd fallen into a steady rhythm that consisted of him pumping into her while she thrust her hips back and forth.

As much as Clint wanted to get her undressed all the way, he wasn't about to take his hands from where they were. Lynn's muscles tensed and tightened around him. Her taut little backside fit perfectly in his grasp, and he never got tired of the powerful way her legs locked around him.

Leaning back a bit, Lynn ground her hips into Clint and held onto him with one hand around the back of his neck.

She wriggled and slid along his hard cock while using her other hand to pull open the front of her dress. The material didn't have much slack, but she managed to open it just enough for Clint to see the erect nipples on her pert breasts.

"You like that, don't you?" she whispered.

Clint nodded and ran his tongue from the exposed skin of her chest up to her neck. "It's like you can read my mind."

Pumping her hips a bit quicker, she rode his cock and said, "I don't need to read your mind. I can feel everything I need to know right here."

Sure enough, Clint was growing harder by the second. Every so often, both of them glanced toward the door, as if expecting to be interrupted at any moment. Although that wasn't a pleasant notion, the possibility got Lynn wetter every time she turned to the door.

"We don't have much time," she whispered.

Clint wrapped his arms around her and thrust all the way inside her. That caused Lynn's eyes to widen and a surprised smile to appear on her face. From there, Clint stood up and carried her right along with him.

As he lifted her off the bed, Clint could feel her entire body trembling against him. Lynn dropped her head so she could moan directly into his shoulder. She made just enough noise for him to hear, but the way her body trembled and her muscles tensed was almost enough to make Clint let out some noise of his own.

Clint walked her to the closest wall, but didn't get there before he felt Lynn grind against him. Cupping her bottom in his hands, Clint helped her ride his cock back and forth while thrusting her hips every so often to get him completely inside.

Lynn locked her hands behind Clint's neck and leaned back as much as she could. Her eyes were clenched shut and her expression was a mix of intense pleasure and concentration. She shifted until she found the exact spot she wanted. Once there, it only took a few more wriggles of her hips to get her trembling again.

For a little while, Clint enjoyed just watching her as Lynn was engulfed by a powerful orgasm. But he couldn't hold himself off too long before pumping in and out of her again. Soon, his knees were turning weak and Lynn was holding onto him so tightly that he didn't even need to support her.

As Clint lowered himself back onto the edge of the bed, Lynn thrust her hips a few more times to push him close to the finish. It was a good thing he was sitting down by the time his climax hit him, because Clint would have been knocked off his feet.

Slowly, Lynn loosened her legs from around Clint's waist and lowered one to the floor. She moved away from him and took a staggering step back from the bed. "I wasn't expecting that," she gasped.

Clint laughed as he stood up and pulled his clothes back on. "That's funny, considering I was about to say the same thing."

She used her hands to straighten her hair and pulled her clothes back into line as best she could. "Actually, I wasn't expecting how I would feel seeing you like that."

"Like what? Bloody and covered in dirt?"

"No," she replied while tracing her fingertips along Clint's chest. "Standing up for me even as a gun's being fired at you."

"In all honesty, your old flame and his friend aren't very good shots."

"Mark wasn't any sort of a flame. At least, not like you mean. And don't make me explain myself too much. It's embarrassing."

Clint moved toward her and placed his hands upon her hips. "You don't have to explain anything," he said. "I think we've been doing just fine as it is."

"Me too."

They kissed once more, but without the fire that had already taken them so far. It wasn't as if the fire was gone, only that neither of them had enough steam left to rekindle it at the moment.

Just then, someone started to turn the doorknob. Whoever it was stopped halfway through and pulled the door shut again. A second later, there was a quick knock.

Lynn smirked as if she was getting away with something and said, "Come on in."

The door was pushed open just enough for Wes to take a look inside. Even so, the farmer kept his eyes aimed more toward the floor than anything else.

"Didn't know if you were decent in there, Lynn," Wes said. "I was just wonderin' if you knew where Clint was."

"I'm right here," Clint replied.

That brought Wes's eyes up, and he glared at Clint as if he was about to skin him alive right then and there. After a few seconds, he shrugged and nodded. "You wanna step outside? We got some things that need to be discussed."

TWENTY-TWO

Wes didn't say a word as he led Clint through the house.

They passed Tina along the way, but she simply waved and gave Clint a concerned smile as he passed by the sitting room. She didn't try to get up, and she looked away before Wes pulled open the side door leading out from the kitchen.

As they stepped outside, the cold night air slapped Clint in the face. After all he'd been through, good and bad, the cool breeze felt awfully good. As Wes paced a bit and then turned to look at him, Clint simply stood and looked up at the clear, starry sky.

Finally, Wes cleared his throat and said, "I knew that girl since she was small."

"You mentioned that."

Wes started to jab his finger at Clint and then let out the breath that had been drawn up inside him. His fist relaxed and he just gave Clint a tired wave. "Ah, don't mind me. I'm just some old dog who's used to baring his teeth at strangers."

"Especially when those strangers come sniffing around your pups, huh?"

Wes smirked and tried not to laugh, but couldn't help

himself. "Yeah, I suppose you're right. No hard feelings, though. I suppose there's no reason why you and Lynn can't do what you please. I think she's sweet on you, so she probably wants to spend more time with you than with me."

Judging by the innocence in Wes's words, Clint figured the walls and door of that room were thicker than he'd thought. After what Wes had just said, however, Clint didn't see any reason why he shouldn't just let that sleeping dog lie.

"You wanted to talk about something?" Clint asked.

Wes stuffed his hands in his pockets and walked over to an old stump. He propped one foot up on the stump and leaned forward so he could gaze out at his land. Clint walked over to stand beside him. The old stump was slanted on one side as if the old man's boots had been there enough times to wear down the wood.

"This here place used to be a mess," Wes said. "Over yonder, there used to be a lake. Before that, the lake used to hook up to the river. It wasn't anything big enough to float a boat, but it was enough to water a couple of fields or turn a mill wheel or two. Leastways, it was until the water was all used up."

"Must not have been much of a river," Clint said.

"No, it sure wasn't. Fact is, it made this whole town stink to high heaven. I bought this farm for a steal, 'cause the old riverbed used to take up a good section of it. More'n half of my property was either mud, rocks or something close to a damned swamp. There was some green to work with, so I bought it up, rolled up my sleeves and got to work."

While he listened to Wes, Clint found himself putting his foot up on the old stump as well. Looking out at the field, he could almost picture the muddy remnants that a dried up pond would have left behind. Because the pond had been connected to a river, there was only that many more things that could have drifted to the bottom for Wes to find.

"How long ago was that?" Clint asked.

"Let's just say I was freshly married and my girl wasn't even a twitch in my trousers." Judging by the guilty look Wes shot back toward the house, he would never have said that if Tina had been within earshot. "It was a hell of a lot of work, Clint. Every farmer worth his salt needs to break his back every day, but this was more work than most anyone else around here wanted to do. But I got this place for a song and I built it up to what you see here."

Clint took a look around, but didn't need to see much to admire what Wes had done. "You did a hell of a good job," he told the farmer.

"Thanks, Clint. I appreciate it."

"Let me hazard a guess about something. You bought this land from a prospector who'd panned the river for years and probably kept panning even when it dried up to a pond."

The smirk was still on Wes's face as he looked over to Clint and nodded. "You're real close. It was a couple prospectors who got into the game way before I decided to settle in these parts. They pulled a fair amount of gold out of the river, but they always thought there'd be more. Hell, I even tried my hand at tin panning, but I never saw the sense in it."

"That's probably because you didn't find anything," Clint pointed out.

"The hell I didn't! I pulled a few nuggets and some dust out of there. How do you think I got started in saving up for this land?" Wes shifted his eyes back to the field and even let them drift up to the sky every so often. "It wasn't much, to be certain, but enough to get me started. The rest of the money I put together with hard work and my own two hands."

"Sounds like prospecting to me."

"Maybe, but the land is sure less fickle than the river. Farming may be hard, but it's steady. It took a long time for me to pull it together, but I got what I needed. All the while, them prospectors said I was foolish. When the river dried up and the time came for them to sell, they approached me first with their hats in hand. I probably could've talked them down on the price, but I didn't have it in me to gouge them any more."

Clint gave Wes a pat on the back. "Good thing you're a farmer. You've got too much of a conscience to be a good businessman."

According to the way Wes laughed, he took that exactly as Clint had intended. "Knowing them fellas, they probably made a fortune somewheres else."

Wes pulled in a deep breath and let it out. It seemed to be an effort, but eventually he said, "I found the first chunk in my pumpkin patch. It was a spot I never planned on doing anything with because the girls used to play there. I had plenty of land, so I left it alone. I was digging there not long ago, hit a rock, pulled it up and damn near threw it into a ditch. When I saw what it was, I about keeled over."

Reflexively, Wes looked over both shoulders. Even though there was nobody else in sight, the farmer still leaned closer to Clint and lowered his voice to a whisper. "I worked with them prospectors. It wasn't for long, but I know how men get when they see that much gold. I didn't want to sell it right away, so I thought I'd break it up and sell it in a few different spots.

"I thought about hauling it into town right here and explaining what happened, but the man who'd do the transaction is new to town. He's from Montana, I think, and I don't trust them folks. Even if the man was honest, there's still a chance of me bein' robbed by someone else who saw what I brought in or how much money I got for it."

Clint would have liked to tell the farmer that he was

being too suspicious, but he knew better than that. The sad truth was that it was always the safest bet to assume the worst from your fellow man. That only went double when there was money involved. Considering the amount of gold Clint had seen, maybe triple.

"I thought about getting rid of it, but that's just silly. I could use that money and it's legally mine. I found the gold on my property!"

Clint held his hands up as if he was surrendering. "No need to convince me. I agree."

The fire in the old man's eyes tapered off. "I thought about giving it to Tina, but she'd probably be robbed quicker than I would. Robbed or . . . or worse. Then I found the second chunk a few yards from where I got the first . . ."

"Wait a minute," Clint said. "The second one? Oh, so there's two piled up under those rags."

Wes shook his head. "That's just one. The third one."

"Good Lord," Clint said.

"Yeah. Now you see my predicament. If I wanted to leave here, I could sell it and move on. I'd have to watch my back for a little while, but I could manage. But I'm too old to just pull up stakes. Besides, I've sunk everything I am into this place. This farm's the blood in my veins and the sweat off my brow. I ain't about to just sell it."

Wincing a bit, Clint said, "Still, you could afford to live in a pretty fancy place. You'd never have to work again."

Wes seemed to consider that for almost an entire second before scowling as if he'd bitten into a rotten apple. "I couldn't live without workin'. It just don't suit me."

"No," Clint replied even though he'd only known Wes for a short time. "It sure doesn't."

"So what the hell am I supposed to do with that gold? Give it away? Sell it off? Either way, I can see the wrong man gettin' wind of it and coming after me for more. I don't want to put my girls into that sort of danger. That is . . . unless they had someone else around to help protect them."

Clint smirked and said, "That's all I needed to hear."

TWENTY-THREE

The room Clint was given was smaller than the one Lynn had used to patch him up. It had all the comforts, but not enough for someone to get too comfortable. The bed was a cot. The chair was straight-backed and without any padding. The only thing hanging from the wall was a circular shaving mirror over an old, empty basin.

If the other room was a reflection of Tina's sensibilities, this one was Wes all the way down to the bare floor.

Clint was able to size the room up in less time than it took for Wes to leave and let him settle in. For Clint, settling in was a simple enough matter. He was finished once he took the saddlebag off his shoulder and draped it over the back of the chair.

Testing the bed with the palm of his hand, Clint pushed on the mattress and heard several squeaks. Only one of them came from the bed frame, while the others came from the floor and door hinges. Clint turned around to find Tina opening the door and looking inside.

"You're staying?" she asked.

Clint didn't answer right away. For a few seconds, he was distracted by how much different she looked in comparison to how she'd looked before. Tina never did look bad, but she looked even better now that she'd changed into a long nightgown and allowed her hair to flow freely over both shoulders.

Tina's hair was slightly shorter than Lynn's and much darker. In fact, her hair was so dark that it made Tina's skin look almost luminescent. The only things to stand out more than her eyes were her full, red lips.

Before staring at her any longer, Clint shook himself out of his state and tried to pass it off with a half yawn. "Sorry about that," he said. "It's been a long day."

"Yeah," she said, obviously not buying his poorly attempted explanation for staring at her. "It has been a long day. So, you're staying on for a while?"

"Just for a little while. Your father asked me to."

Tina had started to turn away from him and took hold of the door frame with one hand. Pausing to give Clint a lingering look at the way the light passed through her nightgown to show the generous curves beneath it, she said, "Good. Because I would have asked if he didn't. It's much too late to push you out into the cold."

"Well, I sure do appreciate it."

Tina was poised with one foot in Clint's room and one foot out of it. She kept one hand resting upon the door frame, while slowly running the other hand up and down a stretch of polished wood.

The longer she stood there, the easier it was for Clint to pick out another subtle detail in the way her nightgown clung to her. After her arm brushed down along her front, her nipples became just erect enough to poke through the single layer of material that was covering her.

"How long will you be staying on?" she asked.

"Well, your father has some work that needs to be done, so I'll probably stay around until that's done."

"You don't look like a farmhand," she said as her eyes worked their way slowly up and down his body. "And you sure don't look like just another cowboy. By the way you handled yourself earlier, I'd say you're some sort of gun-man."

"Gunsmith, actually. It's my trade."

"And that's why you're staying?"

"No," he admitted. "Not exactly."

Tina nodded and slowly turned her back to him. Her hips moved beneath the clean cotton of her nightgown in a way that made Clint want nothing more than to grab hold of them and pull her close.

When she looked over her shoulder once again, Tina's expression made it seem that she could read his thoughts like a book.

"Do you need some blankets?" she asked. "Or anything else to keep you warm tonight?"

Tina may not have been much for understatement, but she was doing a hell of a job on Clint's nerves. Mainly, it was getting more and more difficult for him to keep from grabbing hold of her right then and there. If he hadn't just talked to Wes about what a cute little girl she'd been, Clint wouldn't have had that much control.

"Some blankets would be nice," he said.

She smiled even wider and walked away. A few seconds later, Tina delivered the blankets and gave him a quick "Good night, Clint" before leaving him in peace.

Whether or not anyone else showed up to take a shot at him or steal the gold, Clint knew the next couple of nights would be very interesting.

TWENTY-FOUR

There was a gentle knock on Mark's door around eight in the morning. He started to roll over, but found he couldn't move. As much as he wanted to kick his feet over the side of the bed and open the door, he simply couldn't do it.

The bed was too damn comfortable.

After sleeping on the ground or on a wooden rack covered in stinking rags for so long, Mark had forgotten what it was like to have proper comforts. Since the best he could do was lift his head an inch or so from his pillow, Mark screamed loud enough to make up for his lack of motion.

"What?!" he hollered.

After a brief pause, a meek voice came from the other side of the door. "You said you wanted to know when breakfast was being served," the voice said. "It's being served right now."

Mark grunted a few times and waved off the young woman as if she could see him. When he pulled open the door, he saw a slender woman with short black hair walking away from the door. Once she got a look at him, she hustled even more quickly away from his door.

Still grunting to himself, Mark slammed the door shut and pulled on some clothes. From there, he stepped outside and stomped down the stairs as if he was trying to punish each and every one of them. When he got to the little dining room on the first floor, Mark had to look twice to make sure he was seeing things properly.

"Howdy," Joey said as he waved at him from one of the tables. He wore a sloppy grin on his face and had to break away from one of the three women who were tending to him.

The women might not have been pretty as pictures, but they were all good enough to spark some jealousy when Mark saw how they fluttered attentively around Joey. Jealousy hit even harder when he saw the smiles on the women's faces disappear once they got a look at him.

"I've been up for a while," Joey announced. "You should try the bacon and eggs. They're great."

The shorter of the three women must have also been the cook, because she looked flattered by Joey's words. She even blushed a bit as she reached out to pinch one of his cheeks.

"In case you forgot," Mark grunted as he plopped down onto a chair at Joey's table, "we've got work to do. Or did one of your new lady friends help you out with that too?"

"Not as such, but Katie did tell me which saloon we should stay away from if we wanted to avoid trouble. I think we should try that one first."

"You think so, huh?"

Since Joey was too chipper to pick up on sarcasm, Mark stopped piling it on and turned his glare toward the table. "What the fuck do I need to do to get some breakfast?"

The short woman who before had been so flattered now looked as if she was about to faint dead away. She'd been standing at Mark's left and was just about to introduce herself when he'd let that obscenity fly. After steeling herself with a deep breath, she asked, "What can I get for you?"

"Whatever he's having," Mark grunted. "And be quick about it."

The woman mumbled to herself as she walked away. Although she was careful to keep her voice low, a few choice words managed to drift through the air. If Mark had been listening to her in the slightest, he might have been upset to hear what she had to say. As it was, he was too busy stealing a dirty cup from another table and filling it from the pot of coffee sitting in the middle of his own table.

"Where's that saloon?" Mark asked.

"On the other side of town. It's called the Triple Diamond. If we don't find someone there to suit our needs, we might be out of luck. This is a pretty quiet town."

Mark let out something that was part chuckle and part snort. "I'll say it is. Any place with women who like the looks of you must be backward as all hell."

Joey started to get annoyed, but caught the other two women looking his way. That cheered him up quickly enough and he dug back into his breakfast.

A few minutes later, the short woman came out with the plate holding Mark's breakfast. When she saw him dive right in and start devouring the eggs, the woman smirked and walked away.

"I don't know what the hell you're thinking," Mark said through a mouthful of food. "This tastes like someone wiped the floor with it."

TWENTY-FIVE

Clint had been up since the first of the sun's rays had poked over the horizon. According to Wes, he was allowed to sleep late due to all the commotion from the night before. Oddly enough, Clint didn't feel as if he'd had so much rest.

The first thing Clint thought he'd do was get a look at the gold and try to figure out a better spot to hide it. It was either that, he figured, or try to hatch a good plan for what should come next regarding the windfall. But Wes had other ideas.

Clint's feet had barely touched the floor when he was dragged out by the farmer.

"There's work to be done," Wes had announced.

"I know. If those men decide to come back, we should—"

"Not that kind of work," the farmer interrupted. "Real work. Or have you spent too much time in saloons to remember what that is?"

When he'd pulled in a breath, Clint caught the strong scents of ham, coffee and potatoes. "Smells like breakfast's about ready."

"And it'll be even better once we've worked up an appetite."

Before Clint could let the farmer know that his appetite

was just fine, he was catching the clothes thrown at him and being pulled outside.

"Are you serious?" Clint asked. "Those men might not be crack shots, but they could be coming back."

Wes nodded and kept walking. "Yep."

"They might get some help."

"Could be. They also might be long gone," the farmer pointed out.

"You want to take that chance?"

Wes stopped and turned around with his hands propped on his hips. "Look here, Clint. If I've learned anything, it's that there's a time to reap and a time to sow. If those killers come back, it'll be time to reap. Until then, it won't do nobody any good us just waiting around twiddling our thumbs. Now's the time to sow. That needs doing too, you know."

Within seconds, Clint had an ax in his hand and was chopping firewood. That was fine. He'd done that plenty of times before.

Next, he had to milk the cows. That wasn't too bad. Clint was vaguely familiar with the basics.

Then, there were chicken coops to be mended, more wood to be cut, a fence that needed patching and a plow blade that needed sharpening. None of these things were out of Clint's range, but it had been awhile since he'd had so much thrown at him at such an early hour.

"Don't you fend for yerself when you're out there riding?" Wes asked while tossing the ax into Clint's hands for the third time.

"Sure," Clint replied.

"And you seemed to be plenty able when it came to fighting. Put some of that gumption into honest work."

Clint found himself glaring at the old man. "It's a whole lot easier to get moving when someone's shooting at you. If you'd like to see what I mean, I'd be happy to oblige."

For a second, Wes stood there as if he was too shocked

to move. Some anger flickered across his face, but it was soon replaced by plain old surprise. Then, he started to laugh.

"Aw, hell, Clint. You're funny. You want to go and have something to eat?"

"That would be great."

"You wearing your pistol?"

"No, sir," Clint replied. The absence of that familiar weight at his side had been bothering him all morning.

"Good," Wes said. "Chop that wood first and then you can eat."

Once Clint had gotten some food in his belly, his spirits brightened considerably. Conversation around the table didn't stray too far from the subject of breakfast itself. That, combined with the hard work he'd already done, had a soothing effect on Clint's thoughts. The few words said were cordial. Apart from that, everyone was focused on what they were eating or what chores needed to be done immediately afterward.

One foot in front of the other.

All in all, it was a good way to live.

Eventually, however, the rest of the world barged in and made short work of the peaceful respite they'd been enjoying.

"Come on, Clint," Wes said as he got to his feet. "Let's do that work in the barn I was talking about."

"Did Mark shoot up the barn too?" Lynn asked.

"That's what we aim to find out," Wes replied.

Clint saw Lynn glance nervously at him, but he simply nodded and walked toward the door. She obviously knew there was more to it than that. The anxiousness on her face made that much clear as day. Since there was other work to be done, Clint left her in the house and followed Wes out to the barn.

A time to reap and a time to sow.

Once he caught up to Wes, Clint was inside the barn. The old farmer had a way of moving with his back hunched and his knees buckled while still covering plenty of ground in a short amount of time. When he got a look at the back wall inside the barn, Wes moved even faster.

"What the hell?" he muttered.

"What's wrong?" Clint asked.

"Were you messing with these rags?"

"I told you what I did. I nudged them with my boot, got a quick look underneath and then straightened them again. Why?"

Wes was hunkered down over the pile and fussing with it without disturbing much of anything. "These ain't the way I left 'em is why. They're pushed to one side."

"Are you sure? They look the same to me."

"I know how I left 'em and this ain't it. It's not even close. Hell, you can see some of . . ." Reflexively looking around, Wes straightened the rags and lowered his voice. "I checked on 'em the night before last. Did you poke around here after that first time?"

Clint shook his head. "No, sir."

"Then that means that fella that was in here got a look at this gold."

Recalling that Mark had bolted out of the barn through the back door, which was only a few paces from the rags, Clint felt his gut tighten. "If that's so, then there could be a lot more trouble coming a lot sooner than we thought."

TWENTY-SIX

Mark and Joey had been to some pretty filthy saloons. They'd been to some that had more blood than sawdust on the floor and enough teeth in the spittoons to fill several mouths.

The Triple Diamond wasn't one of those saloons.

While it might have been dirty by Thickett standards, the place was actually quite nice. All of the tables were cleared off. The beer was poured into clean mugs. Even the dancing girls were easy on the eye. It was the only place in town that served whiskey and also hosted round-the-clock poker games, which is what earned it the reputation it had gotten from the more respectable of Thickett's residents.

Mark and Joey stepped into the place and walked up to a bar that might have been polished within the last month. When he saw the barkeep take notice of him, Mark leaned against the bar and glanced at the rest of the folks within the saloon.

"What can I get for ya?" the bartender asked.

"A beer for me and my friend," Mark replied.

After nodding once, the barkeep filled the order and placed the drinks in front of them. "Anything else?"

"Yeah. I need to know where I can find someone to do some work for me."

"What kind of work?"

Although Mark wasn't a notorious bad man, he understood enough of that life to know when he was talking to someone who lived it as well. The bartender wasn't one of those people.

"Never mind," Mark grunted.

The barkeep gave them a friendly smile and stepped back. "You need anything else, just let me know."

"I think we could beat the hell out of the men in this place," Joey grunted. "Where the hell are we supposed to find someone to help us get our hands on that gold you talked about?"

Mark snapped his head around and spoke in a hissing whisper. "I told you not to flap your goddamn lips about that, didn't I?"

"Yeah," Joey said with a nod. "I don't think anyone heard. That is, anyone else but that man over there."

Mark looked in the direction Joey had nodded and found a lone figure sitting at a table. He was dressed in plain clothes that seemed just dirty enough to have covered a few miles of trail. The man's face was calm and decorated with a well-kept mustache. Although he didn't make much of a show of it, he was obviously watching Mark and Joey very closely. There was a confidence in his eyes that didn't waver in the slightest once he'd been singled out by the two men. In fact, it was Joey and Mark who started to look away, when they found themselves under the man's gaze too long.

"You think he knows someone we could use?" Joey asked.

Mark's eyes dropped for a second, but that was just long enough to spot the gun at the stranger's side. When he looked up again, Mark found an intense look on the stranger's face that was more than enough to discourage him from looking any longer.

"Yeah," Mark replied. "I think he might be able to help."

"Then let's go over there."

"We probably shouldn't just—"

Before Mark could finish what he was saying, the stranger pushed his chair away from the table and stood up.

"Can I set you up with anything else?" the bartender asked, immediately seizing the opportunity to be of some use.

"No," the stranger replied curtly. He then headed for the door and flipped a silver dollar through the air. By the time the coin landed on the bar, the man who'd tossed it was halfway outside.

Mark gritted his teeth and choked down the bad feeling that was creeping up into the back of his throat like a wad of bile. "Come on," he said to Joey. "Let's see where he's headed."

The bartender chirped something at them as they stepped outside, but Mark didn't pay him any mind. Instead, Mark searched for the stranger as his hands shot out to hold open the door that had been slammed in his face.

Even though the door stopped short of cracking against the frame behind them, a loud bang echoed through the air.

Mark and Joey reflexively twitched at the noise. When they heard the other bangs follow the first, they backed up until their shoulders knocked against the front of the saloon.

The stranger was a few paces to the left of the door and stepping into the street when Mark spotted him. The stranger's arm was also in motion as it bent at the elbow and raised a .38-caliber Smith & Wesson pistol to hip level. The stranger didn't fire, but the pair of men who bolted into the street were doing more than enough firing of their own.

"The bank's been robbed!" someone shouted from nearby.

Mark and Joey looked at each other, but didn't know what to say. Before either of them could make a noise, the stranger and his two partners had met in the middle of the street.

These two men wore their dusters buttoned up, with the collars flipped, so they were mostly covered from their noses all the way down to their shins. Each of them carried a burlap sack in one hand and a smoking pistol in the other. Turning as they fired, the two men in dusters shot again and again at the small building they left behind.

As the three men met up, a few other men emerged from the bank. Judging by how they fired at the trio in the street, the men coming from the bank weren't friends of the trio.

"Those men robbed the bank!" a man from the bank's doorway shouted. "Someone stop them!"

Mark and Joey stood their ground as more and more hell spilled out around them. More shots were fired. More people were shouting. A few women were screaming. A few more men holding shotguns emerged from even the buildings around the bank and saloon.

"Now's our chance," Mark said. "Just follow my lead." With that, Mark drew his own pistol and took aim at one of the men closest to him.

Even though Joey was clearly surprised by the move, he drew his own weapon all the same.

The stranger from the saloon turned on his heels and took aim at Mark and Joey in as much time as it took to blink. When he saw Mark drop a shotgun-wielding local from a nearby general store, the stranger refrained from shooting Mark.

The man Mark had shot was a potbellied fellow answering the frantic call from the bank. He hadn't even gotten a chance to bring his shotgun up to his shoulder before a round from Mark's pistol caught him in the chest. After that, it was a short fall to the boardwalk.

"Much obliged, partner!" one man in a duster said.

Although a good portion of the outlaw's face was covered by the collar of his duster, he could be seen smiling. He kept his smile even as he took advantage of the chaos surrounding the shotgunner's fall by shooting through the head two of the men still in the bank's doorway.

The other outlaw wearing a duster had rounded up three horses and was bringing them around. He fired every so often, but his shots were randomly placed to just do a good job of keeping the locals away.

"We're coming along with you!" Mark shouted.

The stranger from the saloon shifted a pair of cold eyes to them and asked, "What?"

Mark stood his ground as Joey fired at a pair of men who'd been trying to creep up on the outlaws' flank. Joey didn't drop anyone, but he did manage to clip one in the shoulder.

Climbing into his saddle, one outlaw holstered his pistol and drew another from under his coat. "You keep covering our backs like this and you're more than welcome to tag along. Just be sure you can keep up!"

When he snapped his reins, his two partners followed suit. As soon as their horses got moving, all three men dug their spurs into the animals' sides until they were bolting out of town.

"What do we do now?" Joey asked as he frantically shoved fresh rounds into his pistol.

Mark sent the last of his own bullets flying over the head of the closest local he could find, who just so happened to be the bartender from the saloon he'd just left. "You heard the man," Mark replied as he ran to the post where his and Joey's horses were tied. "Let's tag along!"

As he raced down the street, Mark could see the men that Joey had fired at crawling for cover. The man he'd shot as well as a few lying in front of the bank were obviously never going to move again. All Mark had to do from there was fire a few more shots into the air and watch the other locals scatter as he raced after the bank robbers.

TWENTY-SEVEN

The first thing Clint wanted to do was move the gold. Considering how big the chunk was that was hidden beneath all those rags, it wasn't exactly an easy job.

Clint tried moving it on his own with no luck.

Next, he and Wes tried to move it. All that got them was a matching set of strained backs and sweaty foreheads.

"Jesus," Clint muttered as he straightened up and pressed his hand against the small of his back. "How'd you get this here in the first place?"

The farmer was holding up well for a man his age, but was still doing his fair share of sweating. "I was so worked up when I found it, I damn near pulled my back out of joint trying to lift it onto a wagon. After that, I just tied it to the back and drug it here."

"I suppose it's easier to cover up those tracks than to carry it."

"You're damn right. Why do you think I left it here with nothin' but a bunch of rags to cover it up?"

"I was wondering about that awhile ago. Not anymore."

Wes let out a breath and rubbed his hands together. "Why should we move this thing anyways?"

"Because if Mark saw it, then he knows where it is if he comes back."

"And you think that boy can lift it better than us two combined?"

"No," Clint replied. "But it'd be better all around if he thought it was gone."

Eventually, Wes started to nod. "I suppose so."

"You said there was more gold. Where is it?"

Pausing for a moment, Wes eyed Clint suspiciously. The farmer let out the breath he'd been holding and looked down as if he was ashamed of something that had gone through his mind.

"If you don't want to tell me," Clint said, figuring out what was bothering Wes, "you don't have to. In fact, it could be safer if nobody else knew about—"

"I didn't take it from where I found it," Wes said quickly. Now that the words were out, Wes looked as if a rotten tooth had finally been pulled from its socket. "I've been fighting so hard to keep from telling anyone about it, it gets hard to let go."

"Like I said, you don't have to say anything you don't want to."

"And the fact that you tell me that makes me trust you. Actually," Wes added, "the fact that you mean it carries a lot of weight with me. The biggest chunk is in the pumpkin patch. I was trying to get it out of there when you first rode in."

Clint smiled as he remembered seeing the farmer in the pumpkin patch. "And I thought you were just giving me a sour look because I was a stranger riding along with Lynn."

"Well," Wes added with a snarl, "that's not altogether appreciated either. But Lynn's a big girl now and I'd say she's got a fairly good head on her shoulders. Now are we gonna stand here jawing or are gonna get this thing moved?"

"You say there's a root cellar under the stable?" Clint asked.

Wes nodded. "Not much of one, but it's big enough for this thing. Actually, I dug it there to sock away valuables and such. The way the bank in town is guarded, you'd think they were holding nothing but candy in their damned safe."

Clint let out a tired breath and squatted down on his side of the gold. "All right, then. Let's see if we can't get this moving."

Both of them dug their fingers in as far under the gold as they could. From there, they dug in their heels and looked at each other to make certain they were ready for another try. They nodded, tightened their grip and pushed up with their legs.

Sweat trickled from Clint's forehead as a breath slowly seeped from between his lips. It took a few tries, but they finally managed to get the lump of gold moving from the spot where it seemed to have been embedded into the ground. For every fraction of an inch the gold budged, Clint and Wes had to work until every muscle was on fire.

It felt as if Clint was about to break his back, but he eventually moved the gold enough to shift his fingers a bit lower under the muddy surface. They took advantage of each small movement by pushing harder to get the gold rolling.

After all their work, Clint and Wes got the gold moved six feet onto boards that made up a sled attached to the hitch of two plow horses. It wasn't the prettiest contraption, but the simple sled was strong enough to hold the gold's weight. The horses hitched to the sled shifted uncomfortably as they felt the new weight added.

"Easy, now," Wes said as he walked forward and patted each horse's neck. "If we can lift the damn thing, you two can drag it to the stable."

Clint meant to stop for a few seconds to catch his breath, but wound up taking several breaths and wiping his brow. This time, when he looked out the barn door, it seemed an awfully long way from there to the neighboring building.

"So we hide this one and the rest of it," Wes said. "What then?"

"I'll need to work out a few things with you as far as protecting this farm in case those gunmen come back."

"I been protecting this spread for years," Wes said defensively, "and I know plenty about how to do it."

"How many gunfights have you been through?" Clint asked.

The farmer clenched his jaw and furrowed his brow, but remained quiet for a few seconds. "What do you suggest?"

"I'll make my suggestions after we get the gold moved. After we work out a couple plans, I'll see about tracking down those two gunmen and discouraging them from coming back."

"Seems like one of 'em's just after Lynn, but I suppose that ain't much of a comfort. If he knows about the gold, he'll be back for sure. Maybe we should just get her away from here. It'd be a hell of a lot easier than moving this gold."

"Sure," Clint said with a chuckle. "If she wants to go. Making a woman change her mind when she doesn't want to could make moving this hunk of gold seem like tossing a pebble. Besides, it's going to be a whole lot easier to protect one spot rather than two. Those ladies should just stay put until something changes."

"What ladies might those be?" Tina asked as she walked toward the barn.

TWENTY-EIGHT

Wes moved quicker than a man his age had any business moving when he dashed to the pile of rags in the corner and tossed a few onto the heavy load being hauled by the horses. Clint covered the old man by walking forward and standing in the partially open door.

Smiling easily as she walked toward the barn, Tina leaned to one side in an attempt to get a look past Clint. "You two have been in there a while. Is everything all right?"

"Just earning my keep," Clint replied.

"What were you talking about? I heard something about us ladies."

Clint did some quick figuring in his head to guess how much she could have heard. Since Tina was about ten yards from the barn door, she couldn't have heard much. If she'd been any closer, Clint thought he would have spotted her.

"Your father was just warning me to keep my distance," Clint said with a smirk.

"Well, that shouldn't be too hard. I'm headed into town."

"Into town? What for?"

Even though he'd done his best to try and ask the question as casually as possible, Clint could tell that Tina was suspicious. Perhaps it was the fact that Clint was so tired, but he'd sparked a peculiar glint in her eyes when he'd been trying to steer away from that very thing.

"What are you two doing in there?" she asked.

"Just chores. Look, you shouldn't be going into town. Those gunmen might be waiting to get a shot at you."

"It's not me they're after," Tina replied. "It's Lynn. Besides, Mark Rowlett isn't exactly the smartest man in the world. I should be able to stay away from him if I want."

"How well do you know him?"

Tina grinned and shrugged as if she was thinking back to a private joke. "Pretty well," she said.

The more he heard, the less Clint was concerned about hiding the gold. It seemed Tina was hiding a few things of her own and didn't much care about covering her tracks. "What do you know about all of this?" he asked.

"Just what I said. Mark and his friend are idiots. Just because they're out and about doesn't mean I can't go into town for some flour, sugar and sewing needles."

"You live on a farm," Clint told her in the best stern voice he could manage. "There's plenty to eat around here."

Tina merely crossed her arms and stared at him as if he'd sprouted antlers. "We don't grow sugar and we sure don't grow sewing needles. If you're so concerned, maybe you should come with me."

"That's a good idea," Wes said from behind Clint. "Why don't you go with her?"

"I thought there was still work to be done around here," Clint said.

"I can handle the rest on my own," Wes replied. "Besides, you've got things to tend to in town yourself, don't you?"

Clint could see it was pointless to argue. Tina wasn't about to be swayed, and Wes had the right to handle his gold however he saw fit. "All right," Clint said, stopping just short of throwing up his hands. "Let me get my horse saddled."

"No need," Tina replied cheerily, while spinning toward the stable on the balls of her feet. "Willie and Gert practically climb into their harnesses on their own."

"Take Clint's horse," Wes said quickly. "Willy and Gert got work of their own to do."

Figuring Willie and Gert would be happy to be through with hauling the gold as quickly as possible, Clint saddled up Eclipse in record time and rode the stallion out of the stable. He'd been worried about Tina heading into the barn while he was getting Eclipse, but she was busy saddling up her own horse. Once they were done, they left the stable and rode toward the northern property line.

"This is going to be a quick trip," Clint announced. "And try to stay close to me. I don't want you taking a wrong turn and—"

Tina waved him off with one hand before snapping her reins. "If you want to stay close to me, Mr. Adams, you'll have to earn it."

It was easy work for Clint to catch up to her before Tina made it too far past the fence surrounding the farmhouse. Of course, Tina kept making Clint work to maintain his position all the way into town.

TWENTY-NINE

The town was in sight when Clint saw Tina pull back on the reins. Actually, he knew she'd slowed her horse down when Eclipse nearly ran right over her. Having allowed her to stay ahead so he could keep her in sight, Clint had to act quickly to react when she made a sudden stop. Before Clint could ask what had caused her to slow down, he saw the answer for himself.

Two horses thundered away from town and were headed to the east, one following after the other. Since he couldn't see any flames on or around the horses, Clint had to figure they were running away from something else. There surely wasn't anything in sight worth running to.

"That's Mark!" Tina shouted. Turning in her saddle, Tina looked at Clint with excited eyes and said, "That's Mark! I know it!"

"How do you know?" Clint asked.

"That's his horse!"

Clint's first impulse was to doubt what she was saying, and even ask how she knew what she was talking about with such certainty. Before he could do that, he saw one horse catching up to the other. As far as he could tell, they were the animals used by the gunmen who'd shot up Wes's farm.

"Doesn't look like they're headed for Pa's farm," Tina said.

"Maybe not, but they're going somewhere in a rush."

Tina looked at Clint with a definite spark in her eyes. "You want to chase them down?"

"No," Clint replied, giving voice to the first thing that sprang to mind.

But that answer didn't last long.

After catching sight of those two, it didn't stand to reason that Clint should let them ride away. "Aw hell," he grunted as he snapped the reins. Tina's giggle could be heard even over the sound of her own horse building up speed to stay beside Eclipse.

"We're just going to see where they're headed," Clint said.

She nodded, but didn't take her eyes off Joey's back.

"I'm serious," Clint warned. "You'll do what I say or I'll make certain of it personally."

"I like the sound of that."

They rode for a short while before Clint signaled for them to slow. He pulled back on Eclipse's reins and was relieved when Tina matched his pace.

"All right," Clint said in the lowest voice he could manage. "We don't want to get too close."

"Watch it, Tommy!" someone shouted from Clint's right.

Clint looked toward the sound of the voice, but didn't find Mark or Joey. In fact, when he looked to see where Mark and Joey were, Clint found both of them appearing to be just as confused as he was.

More horses could be heard riding up to them. Clint drew his Colt the second he realized he was being surrounded.

"Double back and head toward town," Clint told Tina.

Tina's smile was gone, but she wasn't exactly panicked. "I'll stay here. I can help."

"Just go back to town, dammit! Your staying alive will be all the help I need."

Although she clearly didn't like it, Tina brought her horse around and pointed its nose toward Thickett. She tapped her heels against the animal's sides, snapped the reins and bolted away from Clint.

Two more riders appeared, but stayed well out of pistol range. The man who'd first showed up wore a duster and had his hat pulled down low to cover up a good portion of his face. One of the other riders was dressed in a similar fashion, but the third looked more like a cowboy. All three of them carried rifles.

Clint evened the odds by holstering his Colt and taking his own rifle from where it hung against Eclipse's side. He managed to clear leather, but wasn't able to bring the rifle up before the riders opened fire.

Several shots ripped through the air, hissing within a foot or so of Clint's head. Most of them didn't get that close, however, so Clint took the time to duck and fire a few shots of his own.

The first round Clint fired got close enough to spook the horse of the closest rider. Since the rider wasn't about to sit still long enough, Clint didn't get the chance to follow up with another shot. As soon as the rider pulled back, the other two moved forward.

There was a lull in the shooting that only lasted long enough for the riders to steady their aim. They pulled their triggers in a deliberate fashion, zeroing in on Clint's position until Eclipse started to get nervous. Since the Darley Arabian wasn't the skittish sort, Clint followed the stallion's lead and picked another spot.

As he moved for the cover of some nearby trees, Clint looked for any trace of Tina. Fortunately, he didn't find any. What bothered him was the sight of Mark and Joey steering their horses back toward town. Before Clint could act on that, he heard one of the riders shout over the gunshots.

"Come along with us," the rider commanded. "We got this one pinned down real good."

Mark seemed reluctant at first. He and Joey kept their eyes on Clint as they carefully urged their horses toward the closest man wrapped in a duster. When he saw he wasn't about to be shot from his saddle, Mark flicked his reins and moved even faster. Joey remained at his side the entire way.

Steeling himself and tightening his grip around the rifle, Clint held the weapon up to his shoulder and got Eclipse moving with a nudge from his knee. The instant he got one of the men in dusters in his sights, Clint heard several more gunshots pop around him.

Lead hissed past him, and one piece even found its mark in a tree trunk less than half a yard from his chest. Since the rifles were going off at a controlled pace that resulted in a continuous wave of lead, Clint had no choice but to move farther back into the trees.

One of the riflemen even got an angle behind those trees, which forced Clint back even farther.

Clint heard one of the riflemen shout something to the others, which was followed by the sounds of several sets of hooves pounding against the dirt. When Clint rode around the trees, they were all gone. There was nothing left for Clint to do besides curse himself for letting someone else get the higher ground.

THIRTY

Clint didn't stop when he got to Tina's side. Instead, he simply reached out to grab her horse's bridle and take it along as he kept Eclipse moving down the street. He was so preoccupied looking for an ambush that he didn't even notice how busy the street was.

Once he reached a corner that put plenty of turns between where he was and the spot he'd left behind, Clint looked Tina over carefully. "Are you all right?" he asked. "Did you get hit?"

"I'm fine, Clint. You still could have killed me by pulling my horse around by the nose like that."

"I thought I told you to get somewhere safe. You were just standing there waiting in the open."

"You told me to get into town. That's where I was and I was plenty safe. Besides, those men didn't even come this way."

"Well, they could have," Clint snapped.

Tina looked as if she was about to say something, but then shifted her eyes away from Clint altogether. With just enough force to get the job done, she turned her horse's head away from him until the bridle slipped from Clint's grasp. "The shop I wanted is right over this way," she said calmly.

Clint followed her, feeling very much like a scolded child. That ended when he got Eclipse to close the distance between him and Tina. Once they were on level ground again, Clint recalled something that had stuck in his head for a while. "You seemed to pick out Mark's horse pretty quickly," he said.

"I was there when they rode onto my farm the other night, remember?"

"Yes, but still. That was in the dark and there was a lot going on at the time. Most folks wouldn't remember something like the horse's breed or color."

Tina shrugged and replied, "I like horses."

"And I'd like you to answer me honestly."

Sighing as she climbed down from her saddle, Tina took her sweet time in tying her horse to a hitching post. Finally, she tossed her hair over her shoulder. "I've seen Mark a few times before. I just didn't want Lynn to know."

"She's not here. You could have mentioned it before."

"She may not be here, but you are," Tina pointed out. "Don't tell me that you and her don't talk . . . among other things."

"And I thought women told each other everything."

"Well . . . mostly everything. Every lady likes to have her little secrets."

Clint had his feet on the ground and was tying Eclipse to the post by now. He cinched in the knot and nodded as he chuckled under his breath. "And I suppose you being with Mark is one of those secrets."

"Among others."

"Why might that be?"

Tina walked along the boardwalk and twirled a finger through a curl in her thick, dark hair. All around her, folks were running from one spot to another and chattering nervously to themselves. Even as she walked close enough to see this, Tina acted as if nothing of interest was happening beyond whatever it was that floated through her mind.

"Lynn and I have always had the same taste in men," Tina said wistfully. "Sometimes our timing isn't quite right."

Although Tina didn't seem to notice the way the locals scurried back and forth across the street, Clint sure did. He could feel the excitement as if it was a static charge hanging in the air after a storm. When he pulled in a deep breath through his nose, he could also detect the hint of burnt gunpowder.

"Are you even listening anymore?" Tina asked petulantly.

Clint put on half a smile and nodded. "Yeah."

Even though the smile was weak, it was good enough for Tina. She looked back to the door she was about to open and stood there with her fingers perched upon the handle. "Would you like to come inside with me?"

"No. I think I'll get something to drink. It looks like there's some sort of commotion around here, so I'll try to find out what it is."

Tina looked around as if she hadn't noticed one bit of the commotion that Clint mentioned. When she did catch sight of the locals bustling about, she shrugged and pulled open the shop's door. "Suit yourself. When I'm done here, I'll go to the general store on the corner."

Clint looked up to see that she was stepping into a seamstress's shop that had some dresses hanging in the front window. "All right. I won't be far."

Practically skipping into the shop, Tina let the door swing shut behind her. That left Clint to his own devices as he walked a few paces down the boardwalk where more of the commotion was taking place.

Even though Clint tried several times to catch someone's attention, the locals seemed as oblivious to him as Tina had been to everyone else. Finally, Clint reached out

with one hand to grab hold of a young man by the sleeve of
his brown suit coat.

"What's going on here?" Clint asked.

The young man was shocked to be caught that way, but
calmed down when Clint let go of his sleeve. "The bank
was robbed," he said in a rush. "Didn't you hear the
shots?"

"I just got into town, but I did cross paths with some
armed men who seemed to be in a big hurry."

"That'd probably be them. They shot the street up,
made off with most of the money in the bank and even
killed three men."

"Jesus."

The young man seemed anxious to leave, so he turned
and started on his way once more.

"Who's the law around here?" Clint asked.

Stopping and turning around again, the young man
seemed almost as surprised as the first time he'd been
stopped. "That'd be Sheriff Copeland."

"Where can I find him?"

"Just follow me. I need to have a word with him too."

THIRTY-ONE

Clint had to be quick to keep up with the young man. Once he saw where the man was going, Clint realized that most of the locals he'd seen were headed that way as well. He barely needed to take half a dozen steps before he could feel himself being swept up into the frantic pace of the crowd.

Before he got too far, Clint stopped and took a look behind him. Compared to what lay ahead, the seamstress's shop seemed calm and peaceful. If the owner of the shop and customers inside were as panicked as everyone else, Clint doubted they would stay in the place. Even so, he figured Tina would be more than happy to be alone to stroll through the shop, looking at the dresses, lingerie, and other items of feminine apparel.

With that in mind, Clint decided to have a word with the town's sheriff and catch up with Tina afterward. From what he'd last seen of Mark Rowlett, Clint wasn't too concerned about that one paying another visit to Thickett anytime soon. In fact, it seemed Mark even had enough on his plate to keep him away from Wes's farm for a good while.

Fortunately, Clint didn't have very far to walk. All he needed to do was round the closest corner before getting a good look at the center of the storm that had been brewing in town. At least two dozen people were gathered around a pair of men who looked as if they were trying to talk to every one of them at once.

Like smaller clouds swirling around the main storm, several other locals talked to one another and vied for attention from the two in the middle of it all. These two men had their hands full, but one of them in particular seemed to be getting pulled in different directions.

As Clint got closer, he could see the badge pinned to the two men's chests. As he'd expected, the busier of the two was the sheriff and the other one was a deputy. Now that Clint was a part of the crowd, he was able to get close enough to make out what some of these folks were saying.

"Where's my money?" someone asked. "It can't just be gone!"

Another voice chimed in. "Yeah! There's got to be a way to get it back! What are you doing here when those men rode off?"

"Men were killed, Sheriff! What're you doing about that?"

"First I need someone to tell me where they went!" the sheriff replied.

"I already told you where they went! They headed east!"

"The hell they did," someone else replied. "They headed north. I seen 'em!"

"They went northwest."

"No, Sheriff! They went southeast!"

In the space of a few seconds, Clint felt as if he was the one being pulled apart by the crowd. At the very least, he could understand why the lawman looked so frazzled.

"Sheriff Copeland will go after those men when he knows where they're headed," the deputy shouted. "That's why we're here to try and figure out where to start."

"They were headed east." Clint said.

Since he wasn't one of the people who'd been shouting

before, Clint's voice caught the attention of both lawmen. When they looked at him and found an unfamiliar face, they kept their attention on him for a bit longer.

"Who might you be, mister?" the sheriff asked.

Clint shoved his way through the crowd so he could get close enough to speak without shouting. "The name's Clint Adams, and I crossed paths with the men you're after on my way into town. At least, I'm pretty sure it was them. Two wore long coats and the rest had guns. They were in a mighty big hurry and took a few shots at me before riding off."

"Sounds like them," the sheriff said as he pushed through the folks standing between him and Clint. Without slowing down, the lawman took hold of Clint's shoulder and guided him to the other end of the crowd.

As he and Clint emerged from the middle of the crowd of people, Sheriff Copeland was snagged by a few who started to fight to regain his attention. All the lawman had to do was nod toward his deputy in order to get the younger lawman moving.

"All right," the deputy said. "That's all for now. The sheriff can talk to the rest of you in his office."

Even though the deputy was keeping them back with a pair of thickly muscled, outstretched arms, some of the crowd wouldn't be dissuaded. None of them got more than a few words out before the deputy raised his voice to an authoritative bark.

"I told you all to clear out!" the deputy said. "And I mean it!"

Although they were anxious to be heard, none of the members of the crowd were anxious to cross the deputy. They backed away and grumbled to one another. That was good enough for Clint and the sheriff to walk down the boardwalk in some semblance of peace.

For the next few steps, the sheriff seemed to be more interested in taking a few uninterrupted breaths than in speaking with Clint. Copeland was a tall fellow who wore his jeans and plain white shirt as if they'd been specially tailored just for him. Every hair on his head was in place and every whisker in his pencil-thin mustache was perfectly aligned. All in all, he looked like the ideal sheriff for a town like Thickett.

"So you say you saw these robbers?" the sheriff asked.

Clint nodded. "Yes, sir. They were riding east."

"Do you know where they were headed?"

"Not exactly, no. But you might want to know that one of the nearby farmers may be in a bit of trouble since—"

"Farmers aren't my concern," Sheriff Copeland interrupted. "Right now, I've got more than enough on my plate without worrying about farmers."

"Actually, those men might come after this farmer."

"And they might come after anyone else. What I need to do is form a posse and get those men into my jail. Once that's done, they won't be bothering anyone, farmers or otherwise. Unless you want to ride on a posse, you'll have to save whatever else you wanted to say for another time."

Clint hooked a thumb over his gun belt and stood so that he forced the sheriff to stop and listen when he said, "All you need to do is swear me in."

Copeland paused for a second to look Clint over. When he saw the modified Colt at Clint's side, he nodded and told him, "You're sworn in. Now get a horse and be back at this spot within the hour."

Glancing at the spot Copeland had mentioned, Clint saw a sign over the closest doorway, which marked the building as the sheriff's office. When Clint looked back again, Copeland was gone. Rather than try to chase after the lawman, Clint hurried to the seamstress's shop where he'd left Tina. She was still in the back of the store, poking through the finished goods as if it was just another quiet Sunday afternoon. Clint rushed up to her and started explaining what had happened.

"You're going where?" she asked once she snapped out of a daze.

"I'm riding on a posse after Mark and those gunmen," Clint said instead of repeating the entire last half of what he'd already told her a minute ago. "Just stay here until I get back. If I'm gone past nightfall, then stay at a hotel here in town. Just don't ride all the way back to your farm by yourself."

"But it should be perfectly safe to—"

"Do not," Clint snapped, "ride back on your own!"

Tina shrugged and got back to her shopping as though Clint had simply disappeared from her sight.

A second later, Clint truly did disappear—through the front door of the shop.

THIRTY-TWO

Mark had heard about folks who had been sucked up by a twister and thrown into the air, never to be seen again. He'd heard about them just like he'd heard about folks who'd been eaten by wolves or stung to death by bees.

Heard about them, but never met one.

Now Mark knew all too well what it felt like to be picked up and tossed straight into the air. Sitting with his back pressed against a rock and his eyes clenched shut, he was getting a real good notion of what it must have felt like to be kicking and flailing in midair, not knowing where the hell he was or where the hell he was going to land.

One thing was for certain. He didn't like it.

"Ain't nothin' in the world can beat this, huh?"

The words drifted into Mark's ears like something he remembered from a dream. It was a lot of work, but Mark was eventually able to peel his eyelids apart enough for him to get a look at who'd asked that question.

The face Mark saw was mostly covered by a wild beard sprouting from it like shrubs that had taken over an abandoned yard. The eyes staring back at him from over the beard weren't much better. In fact, the eyes were even wilder.

"You got that right," Mark wheezed.

The man with the wild eyes nodded and cleared his throat. The sound turned into a grunting laugh as he lifted his hand to bring a Spencer rifle up closer to his face. "I can feel 'em comin' just as sure as I feel this cold ground against my backside."

Mark looked down as if to make sure the ground was underneath him as well. It sure was. There was also a large rock against his shoulders and something crawling through his hair. Even though he could feel the insect's legs grating against his scalp, he didn't dare move to swat it away.

The stranger from the saloon was on Mark's left and the man with the wild eyes was to his right. Joey and the other man in the duster were lying on their bellies in the middle of some tall grass less than ten yards away. Pressing his head against the rock, Mark was able to see the horses lying down as well. The stranger from the saloon had a tight grip on three sets of reins, forcing the animals to lie down as close to the ground as possible. The remaining horses were held by the man who was also keeping Joey in his place.

"I don't believe I caught yer name," the wild-eyed man said.

It took a moment for Mark to realize that he was expected to answer. When he did, it was in a shaky, unsteady voice. "M-Mark Rowlett."

"Hey there, Mark. I'm Tommy Smalls and that's Vincent."

The stranger from the saloon nodded once to acknowledge the introduction.

"That fellow over there is John," Smalls continued. "At least one of 'em is. Who's the other one?"

"Oh," Mark gulped. "That's Joey."

Smalls nodded as if that little bit of information was all he needed to know about either of the two strangers who were hiding with him behind the rock. Suddenly, Smalls twitched and stretched to look around the rock. When he settled back into his original spot, he was grinning from ear to ear.

"How many men you killed, Mark?" Smalls asked.

"I don't rightly know."

"Sure you do. My guess has the number at somewhere between two and five. You got the look of a man who's handled a gun and has gotten into a scrap or two, but you still needed to check twice to see if you'd really done the deed when you shot that fella back in town. That means you ain't seen enough death to be comfortable with the sight of it. Am I right?"

Smalls couldn't have been more right if Mark had told him what to say beforehand. Even so, Mark did his best to keep his face calm and his voice steady when he replied, "Close, I guess."

"You hear that, Vin? He says I was close."

This was the first time Mark had seen the stranger from the saloon crack a smile. Being on the receiving end of that smile wasn't an enviable spot.

"You hear that, Mark?" Smalls asked, dropping his voice to a chilling whisper. "Them laws are coming just like I said they was."

"We've been waiting here long enough," Mark said as he started to feel his nerve return. Once the sound of approaching horses reached his ears, he shrank right back against the rock. "Jesus. You're right."

"Damn straight, I am. Now let's see if you and your friend are worth keeping around or if we'll all be better off digging a hole and burying you in it."

THIRTY-THREE

It didn't take long to form the posse. Clint had seen some sheriffs take upward of several days to a week to pull together enough men to go after a group of armed killers without getting their heads blown off in the process. Sheriff Copeland managed to gather half a dozen able-bodied men within minutes after Clint rode Eclipse back to the lawman's office.

The confidence the sheriff inspired lasted right up until Clint followed the posse out of town and onto a trail that led up into a rocky pass.

"I don't see anyone, Sheriff," the deputy announced. "Should we turn back?"

The question didn't bother Clint nearly as much as the answer that came soon.

After a bit of deliberation, the sheriff replied, "I don't know. Perhaps we should."

"Perhaps we should?" Clint asked. "What did you expect to find? Those robbers standing out here waiting to be dragged into a cell?"

Sheriff Copeland glared at Clint for a few seconds and then shifted in his saddle as if he was looking for that very thing. When he didn't find it, he said, "No, but I can't exactly ride off and leave the town to fend for itself."

"Do you folks get a lot of men like those bank robbers passing through?"

"We most certainly do not."

"Then odds are you won't get anything much worse than them in the time it takes to do some proper tracking."

Although it was difficult to argue with that logic, the rest of the posse sure seemed as though they wanted to try. Some of them looked away rather than look at Clint, while a few even glanced longingly back at town.

"We'll ride east for a few more miles, fan out and then head back," Copeland announced. "If we don't find them, then they're probably gone and not coming back."

"And what about the men who were killed?" Clint asked. "You think that's enough to answer back for those men getting shot in your jurisdiction?"

Copeland fiercely fixed his eyes on Clint. "If those men are much farther out than a few miles, they're no longer in my jurisdiction. I could hunt them down to the end of the earth, but that doesn't mean I could arrest them."

This time, Clint was the one who was at a loss. As much as he hated to admit it, the lawman had a point. What made it so tough to swallow was how quick all the posse members were to accept it just so they could get home before their dinners got cold.

"Are we at least going to get moving again before those men get any farther away?" Clint asked.

The sheriff nodded solemnly. "Of course. That's why we're here."

Before anyone could snap their reins, another voice made itself heard from among the posse. "They're probably already long gone by now," it said. "We chased 'em off. Ain't that good enough?"

Sheriff Copeland turned in his saddle so he could get a good look at the man who'd spoken. "Most men know they're gonna be chased when they tear out like that. One or two of them might have even caught some lead along the way, which means they'll have to stop and lick their wounds. Either way, they could still be nearby, so shut your mouth and do the job I swore you in to do!"

After that, nobody else among the posse wanted to say a thing.

They rode ahead for a few more miles and kept on going. Even after Clint was certain they'd reached their limit, Copeland led them farther along the eastward trail. Considering they didn't have a tracker along for the ride, Clint soon began to think that there was no real reason for them to continue riding.

It was always painful to admit when the naysayers had it right, so Clint kept his mouth shut and his eyes open.

As they approached a fork in the trail that was marked by some tall grass and a cluster of large rocks, Clint came to a realization: the sheriff may have wanted to catch up with the gunmen, but his posse wanted nothing to do with them.

The men who had been sworn in barely seemed to take their eyes from the trail ahead of them. Every last one of them flinched when they caught sight of a critter scampering across the trail or of a bird been flushed from its hiding spot, but none of them made a real reach for their weapons. In fact, Clint was convinced more than half of the men would have shot off a toe or killed their own horse by accident if they'd tried to clear leather.

Sheriff Copeland led the men toward the rocks as Clint rode up alongside him.

"Hold on a moment, Sheriff," Clint said.

Copeland signaled for the others to stop, and the posse was more than happy to oblige. "What's on your mind?" Copeland asked.

"Maybe we should fan out and circle around toward town. There's not much else this way beside more trail."

"Yeah," one of the posse members eagerly added. "If they was out here, we would have seen those bastards by now."

Surveying the land in front of him, Copeland nodded slowly. "I guess you're right. Half of you men circle around to the north and the other half will circle to the south. All of us will make our way back to town and fire a few shots into the air if you spot the robbers."

Clint led some of the men to the south as if he was herding sheep. "I'll take this group and you can take the other."

"Fine. Let's get moving."

Smalls peeked around the rock and started laughing under his breath. "Looks like them laws are dumber than I thought. They're close enough for me to spit on and they're heading back."

"Should we finish them off?" Vincent asked.

After a bit of consideration, Smalls shook his head. "Nah. Let's just get back."

Mark let out the breath he'd been holding and felt his heart start to beat again inside his chest. Seeing the lawmen actually turn and leave before taking the few more steps that would have sparked another gunfight made him feel like the luckiest man alive.

"What about these two?" Vincent asked as he fixed his eyes on Mark.

When Smalls looked at Mark again, he had the same coldness in his eyes as Vincent. Actually, the coldness Smalls showed was tempered with a bit of wildness that made it even more unsettling.

"They're comin' along with us," Smalls declared. "They did a good job of covering our backs. Besides, it ain't like we can just let 'em go."

"We could always leave them here," Vincent offered. "That way, they won't say anything to anyone."

"When you hear about the deal I can offer you men," Mark sputtered, "you'll be glad to have us along."

Smalls bared his teeth in a wolfish grin. "We'll just have to see about that."

THIRTY-FOUR

Having taken a roundabout way to get back to town, Clint found Sheriff Copeland to be just short of agreeable when he returned. The lawman stood outside his office with his arms folded sternly across his chest. Upon seeing Clint riding down the street, Copeland marched straight ahead to meet him.

"Where the hell have you been?" Copeland demanded.

Clint looked around just to make sure the sheriff was addressing him. "Was I supposed to report for duty? I thought I was just a member of a posse."

"You ain't even that anymore. There is no posse."

"Fine. Then I'll be on my way."

Copeland hopped to the side so he could stay more or less in front of Clint. "The rest of the men already came by to collect their fees. I didn't see you among them."

"Keep the fee," Clint replied.

"That isn't exactly what concerned me. It seems you went off on your own."

Clint sighed and weighed a few options in his head. Since he and the sheriff were the only ones on the street, Clint met the lawman's gaze and lowered his voice a bit. "That posse you rounded up was a joke."

138

"Those men ride along with me whenever I need help."

"And I'm sure they're quick to collect their fee. Have they ever caught anyone?"

"What's that supposed to mean?" Copeland asked.

"Just what I said. They didn't look too anxious to actually confront anyone out there. If they'd ridden far enough to meet up with anyone, I'd say most of them would have been killed right then and there."

Although the sheriff wasn't happy to hear that, he wasn't about to refute it. Finally, he had to choke back his anger and let out an exasperated breath. "They're not gunfighters, that's for certain."

"Maybe you should think about hiring another deputy or two. Even if you narrowed your sights to a few men who could handle themselves in the event of actually stumbling onto an armed man, you might have a good posse. It defeats the purpose if you just bring along a bunch of cowards who are more ready to head home than to do the job they were hired for."

"You're right. Truth is, this town hasn't really seen the likes of those gunmen. There wasn't even much to rob from the bank." Narrowing his eyes a bit, Copeland added, "But if you saw something out there, your duty as a sworn member of that posse is to tell me what it was."

Clint took a moment to consider that and finally nodded. "You're right, Sheriff. I think I saw some men lying in some tall grass not too far from where I had us stop and turn around."

"And you didn't say anything?"

"No, sir. That would have led to shots being fired, and I wasn't about to have something like that happen when I was surrounded by the likes of that posse. Frightened men with guns are more dangerous than a burning powderkeg."

Copeland let out a sigh and ran his fingers through his perfectly clipped hair. "As true as that may be, those men could have been the ones who killed the locals during the robbery."

"And they could have killed you or any number of the posse members before it was done."

"Are you certain about that?"

"Yes, sir," Clint replied without batting an eye. "I am."

"Well, you seem pretty knowledgeable about such things. Couldn't you have done something against a few men lying in the grass?"

"I only caught a glimpse of one or maybe two men lying in hiding in a perfect spot for them to start picking targets off with a rifle. That posse of yours rode up and were shouting back and forth loudly enough to let the whole world know they were coming. What surprises me the most is that the men in the grass didn't pick off a few of us before we got that close."

"Maybe they were just waiting to see if we'd spotted them," Copeland offered.

"My thinking exactly."

"I'm still not comfortable with letting them go like that."

"Neither am I," Clint replied. "But, as a friend of mine recently reminded me, there's a time to reap and a time to sow. That wasn't the time to reap."

"But what were we sowing?" Copeland asked.

"A little confidence. You'd be surprised how much damage a little confidence can do to a reckless man."

"I guess you're right. It would have been nice to catch them, though."

"They'll be caught, Sheriff. Don't worry about that." After tipping his hat, Clint steered Eclipse toward the corner. He then snapped his reins and headed toward the seamstress's shop.

Copeland watched Clint go as his deputy stepped up next to him.

"That the man who was missing from the posse?" the deputy asked.

"Yes, it was."

"He tell you where he went after leaving all the others?"

"No."

The deputy stood in the doorway and watched until Clint rounded the comer and disappeared from sight. "Something about him don't seem right."

"Maybe, maybe not. Don't concern yourself with it too much, though. You need to look for some more men to ride with us when we head back out after those killers."

"Should I round up the boys we normally use?"

Copeland gritted his teeth and shook his head. "No. See what Mr. Lockley and his son are doing. They served in the Federal Army. I'm going to see about hiring another deputy to help out full-time."

"I bet I could get the regular boys a lot quicker."

"I'm sure you can. Just do what I told you, all right?"

THIRTY-FIVE

Tina was sitting on a small bench outside the seamstress's shop when Clint rode up and brought Eclipse to a stop in the street. She took her sweet time getting up and made sure to sigh loudly enough for him to hear as she made her way to her horse.

"The shop's been closed for hours," she announced.

"Then why didn't you go to the hotel? I'm sure it's a lot more comfortable than sitting on a bench."

"Because I hoped you'd be back before I needed to do that. Daddy's probably worried sick."

"Well, I'm here," Clint said. "Let's go home."

Reaching up to grab the saddle horn, Tina put one foot in the stirrup and then stopped. She looked over at him and asked, "Isn't it a bit late to be riding all the way home?"

"It's not that far."

"We could still stay in the hotel, you know."

"We?"

"Sure," Tina replied with a little smirk. "No need for you to sleep outside when I'm all cozy in a warm bed."

She managed to put a bit of a purr into her voice that ran through Clint like soft fingertips along his back. He would have been lying if he told her the offer wasn't tempting.

Then again, he figured that saying anything along those lines would only cause Tina to up the ante. Clint knew himself well enough to be certain he wouldn't last long under such circumstances.

"We need to get back to your farm," Clint said. "Wes is going to be worried and the bank robbers aren't caught yet."

"Bank robbers?" Tina asked casually.

"Don't tell me you were here this whole time and you didn't know the bank was robbed before we arrived?"

"Oh, that's right," she said under her breath as she slid her foot a bit deeper into her stirrup. "I did hear something about that. If they're out there, perhaps it would be better for us to stay put. At least, until morning."

"No. We should be heading back."

Pausing after lifting herself up halfway into the saddle, Tina let her other leg dangle before swinging it over her horse's back. Even though she wore a dress that covered her down to her ankles, the position she was in gave Clint a lingering view of the curve of her back and the inviting roundness of her backside. "Are you sure about that?"

"Yes, Tina," Clint forced himself to say. "I'm sure."

"It seems like someone else thinks differently."

Before Clint could ask for an explanation, he saw Sheriff Copeland round the corner on his horse. The lawman fixed his eyes on Clint and rode directly to him.

"Mr. Adams," Copeland said. "I've taken everything you said under consideration and I agree with you wholeheartedly."

"Thanks. I'm glad I could help."

"You can help by riding with me now as we make one more attempt at trying to track those killers down."

"It's a bit dark for that now, isn't it?"

"Maybe, but time is of the essence," Copeland said. "Since the hour's getting late, the killers are probably trying to find a place to make a camp, and that means they could make a fire. Even if they don't, they can't get too far, which means we should be able to catch up to them."

Looking back at Tina, Clint said, "I have other commitments. I was just about to accompany this lady back to her home."

"Good evening, Miss Petrowski," Copeland said. "If you'd like, I could send someone to tell your father you're in safe hands. As far as that goes, I could just have some of the boys escort you back to your property."

"If Clint's not going back, then neither am I," Tina said. "I think I'll stay in the hotel."

Copeland shrugged. "That'd be fine. I'll even arrange for you to spend the night for free. That is, if Clint decides to help me follow his own advice."

Clint looked at the smug little grin on Tina's face and had to laugh. "Looks like you've got me. Do you think one of your boys would mind keeping an eye on the Petrowski farm for the night?"

"You expecting trouble?"

"Not as such, but there are killers on the loose. If your boys are headed out that way to tell Wes what's going on, then one could stay and see that Wes doesn't get introduced to the killers if we flush them out."

"I'll send my deputy," Copeland said. "That is, if you'd help me again."

"Let's get going," Clint replied. "No use wasting time."

"All right then," Tina said. "You'll know where to find me, Clint."

THIRTY-SIX

Clint returned well after midnight and rode directly to the only hotel in town. Like most everything else in Thickett, the hotel was perfectly maintained and very tidy. The register was aligned with the edge of the desk so well that Clint didn't want to touch it as he looked for Tina's signature.

"Mr. Adams?" the fellow behind the front desk asked.

"That's me."

"I saw you with Sheriff Copeland. Did you find the killers?"

Clint shook his head. "Nope, but we searched the area well enough to know they're long gone. I can only think of a few places that are close enough for them to rest up while staying hidden. They'll be caught before you know it."

"Splendid," the clerk said with a beaming smile. "You'd be looking for Miss Petrowski's room?"

"That's right."

"She's expecting you. It's number four at the end of the hall. Here's the spare key."

Clint took the key that was handed to him, but didn't walk away just yet. "Has there been anything else happening here in town?"

"Not any more shootings, if that's what you mean. No, it's been nice and quiet."

Since he was too tired to keep the conversation going, Clint walked down the hall and stopped in front of the door marked with a large number four. He fit the key into the lock and pushed the door open. It swung on well-oiled hinges, allowing Clint to walk into a good-sized room that was lit by a single candle.

Tina lay stretched out on the bed wearing nothing but a thin white slip. The flickering light coming from the single candle danced along the ample curves of her body in a way that made every shadow look like it was caressing her.

She slowly shifted until she was on her stomach and facing the door. "I've been waiting up for you," she said while brushing the hair from her face.

"I hope you didn't get too comfortable. We're leaving."

Tina's head snapped up and her eyes widened. "What? But it's the middle of the night."

"And I know for a fact the trail's clear. We can get back to your farm with enough time to get a few hours of sleep."

For a few seconds, Tina just stared at Clint as if she was expecting him to do a dance for her. Then, while shaking her head, she slowly began to crawl off the bed. "You're really going to drag me out of here, aren't you?"

"Yep."

"Really?"

Clint grinned and bent down to pick up the dress that was lying on the floor. "I can think of plenty other things I'd rather be doing, but we really need to get going." Before she could say another word, he added, "Really."

Tina snatched the dress from Clint's hand and pulled it on over her head. "Fine. I just hope you know what you're missing."

"Believe me, I've been thinking about that quite a bit."

Once she'd gotten the dress on, Tina straightened it and made sure it was properly tied and buckled in all the right places. The expression on her face was a bit softer when she looked at him again. "I heard all about what happened with those robbers. You're truly brave for chasing after them like that."

"Let's just get going before I have to drag myself along with you out of this room."

Seeing the torture she was inflicting upon Clint seemed to cheer Tina up. She took no small amount of pleasure from bending slowly at the waist to pick up her boots and then allowing her skirt to fall away to reveal a generous portion of her legs while lacing up the boot. "You really are missing a lot, you know," she whispered.

Clint's eyes wandered from the arch of Tina's foot, all the way along the slope of her calf and up to the creamy skin of her supple thigh. As he looked at her, Clint saw Tina's leg open just a little bit before being lowered to the floor so she could stand upright.

"I know," he said breathlessly. "Believe me, I know."

THIRTY-SEVEN

Because she knew the way back home so well, Tina was able to lead Clint straight through a dark, moonless night. All he had to do was keep Eclipse fairly close to her horse and they always had level ground beneath them.

Once they arrived at the farm, Clint signaled for Tina to stop before getting too close to the house, barn or stable. "Stay here for a moment," he said. "I want to make sure everything's all right."

Tina let out a heavy sigh, but did as Clint asked.

Clint flicked his reins, which got Eclipse moving at a decent pace that didn't make too much noise. Now that Clint's eyes had become adjusted to the dark, he could see well enough to know if someone was lying in wait in the vicinity.

A quick circle around the house, barn and stable showed Clint that everything seemed to be pretty much as he'd left it. Nothing was burning and all of Wes's things were in their place. Considering how well organized the old farmer was, that was saying plenty.

Knowing that Tina was watching him, Clint motioned for her to come with him and put the horses in the stable. When he got to the stable door, Clint jumped from his saddle and took hold of the reins so he could lead Eclipse inside.

Tina rode straight into the stable as soon as the door was open. Once inside, she swung down and marched directly at Clint.

Clint heard the steps coming his way, but was still surprised when he turned around to find Tina bearing down on him with such force. "Whoa," he said as he braced himself for the impact. "What are you doing?"

The question had barely passed Clint's lips when Tina walked straight into him and shoved him into one of the two empty stalls. Clint tried to keep his footing, but was stumbling backward too quickly to keep it for very long. When his heel knocked against a floorboard and he started to fall onto a pile of hay, Tina was still right on top of him.

They landed in the hay awkwardly, but with more than enough padding to keep either of them from getting hurt.

"What do you think you're doing?" Clint asked.

Tina's hands were all over him, pulling his shirt, tugging his belt and touching him anywhere she could find bare skin. "You know damn well what I'm doing," she replied. "And I'll stop if you want me to."

"Don't you think . . . I mean . . . what if . . ."

"Just say the word," Tina said as she pulled Clint's jeans down, "and I'll stop."

She stayed still for a moment with one hand on Clint's leg and the other wrapped around his growing erection. The longer Clint went without being able to form a word, the wider she smiled. "Didn't think so," she said.

Clint looked around at the stall. Like most everything else on the farm, it was immaculately clean. Even the pile of hay they'd found had been perfectly shaped. The gate at the front of the stall was just over waist high, which meant Clint couldn't see anything beyond it from his spot on the floor.

It was quiet and dark enough to make it seem like they

were the only two people on the entire farm. As if to chase away the last of his reservations, Tina's lips wrapped around the tip of his cock and slid all the way down to its base.

"Good Lord." Clint sighed as he let his head rest back against the hay.

He could feel her lips tightening around him as her head started to bob up and down. As she sucked him faster, Tina ran her hands up over Clint's chest and then raked her nails gently over his stomach. Soon, she was licking him like she would a stick of candy and humming contentedly all the while.

Clint leaned back and savored the feel of her lips running up and down his penis. He ran his fingers through her hair until he was brought to the height of his pleasure. And, just before he was pushed over the edge, he closed his fist around some of her hair and eased her back.

Tina's eyes widened, and she allowed herself to move however Clint wanted her to move. She watched him intently as he reached out with his other hand to grab her by the wrist. When Clint pulled her down with him, Tina let out an excited breath.

"My, my," she said as she landed on the hay and twisted around so she could look up at him. "What have we here?"

Clint was on his knees with his back straight so he could look down at her. Reaching out to unbutton the front of her dress, he said, "Maybe I should just have a look for myself."

He got the front of her dress open halfway before he simply pulled it off of her. Tina gasped at the rough feel of his hands, but didn't complain in the slightest. In fact, she wriggled her shoulders and arms so she could make Clint's task a little easier. When he placed his hands upon her large breasts, Clint felt Tina's body practically melt.

While leaning down to kiss her, Clint slid his hand up along her leg and under her skirts. Tina slipped her tongue into his mouth and moaned silently as his hand got higher and higher up along her thigh. By the time his fingers were drifting through the downy hair between her legs, Clint felt Tina's chest heaving against him with one labored breath after another.

When he'd started to touch the smooth skin of her inner thigh, Clint had intended on savoring that moment as well. But the more he touched her, the harder it was to hold himself back. He could feel Tina straining against him as well. Her muscles twitched beneath her skin as if every part of her wanted to wrap around him.

Clint's fingers glided along the wet lips of her pussy and then eased their way inside. Her body was hot and moist. He barely got inside of her before Tina was arching her back and letting out a strained moan.

"Don't make me wait any longer, Clint," she begged. "I want you so bad."

By the time she'd finished that sentence, Clint was gathering her skirts up around her waist. Tina spread her legs and wrapped them around him so she could pull him closer. Once Clint felt the tip of his cock brush against her dampness, he thrust his hips forward and buried himself inside of her.

She felt so good that he forgot about everything else. All Clint could focus on was the way Tina's muscular legs locked around him and the way her arms were clamped around the back of his shoulders. Her entire body bucked in time to the pumping of his hips. Her small nipples grew hard the moment he touched them.

And just when he thought it couldn't get any better, Clint felt himself beginning to slip from the pile of hay.

Tina's eyes snapped open and she quickly reached out to steady herself as her body also took the short slide to the floor.

Both of them laughed for a bit as they regained their balance and straightened out the tangle of arms and legs.

By the time he got himself upright again, Clint swore he'd heard every move he made echoing within the stable.

"Maybe we should call it a night before your father comes in here," Clint said. "He may just let his shotgun do his talking before he says a word."

Tina crawled on the floor until it looked as if she was going to use the hay to pull herself to her feet. But rather than climb up, she buried her hands into the hay and leaned forward while arching her back. "You sure you want to leave so soon?"

Clint let his eyes wander along the curve of her back and the rounded lines of her buttocks. "I guess all good things come with a bit of risk attached," he said.

"That's what I like to hear."

Grabbing her by the hips, Clint entered her from behind and pumped into her a few times before his knees began scraping against the rough wooden floor. He backed up and stood before offering a hand to Tina. She looked disappointed at first, but then she hopped into his arms the moment she had her legs beneath her.

Clint caught her and held her up just long enough to feel her legs wrap around him. He backed her up against the rear wall and cupped her backside using both hands. Tina reached down between them and guided his rigid cock into her. All Clint had to do was thrust his hips forward and he was back in business.

It was a good thing that Tina was so petite, because she bounced and writhed against him as he pounded into her over and over again. Before long, it seemed as if they were doing a dance up against that back wall. When the dance was over, both of them were panting breathlessly and clinging to each other in the dark.

THIRTY-EIGHT

Although he hadn't ridden far, Mark Rowlett felt as if he'd dragged himself a hundred miles by the time Smalls called for everyone to stop. They'd arrived at a small trading post a few miles east of Thickett. Mark hadn't even known the place was there and hadn't heard a word about it from anyone in the area. Once he and the rest of the men rode a bit closer, he realized why it was such a secret.

By the looks of it, the place might have been a fort at one time. There was a small cluster of shacks surrounded by the remains of a wall made up of warped, rotting timber. Although there was a main gate, there were at least half a dozen other gaps in the wall big enough to drive a wagon through.

Only a few of the existing shacks appeared safe enough to use. Smalls led the way past a corral and what looked to be a storefront. The only other shack that showed any signs of life was teeming with some of the mangiest whores Mark had ever seen. Considering how he spent his time when he was away from Lynn, that was saying quite a bit.

"There's my girl!" Smalls shouted and pointed to a fat redhead with teeth that would have been more comfortable in a horse's mouth.

The redhead smiled and strutted over to the edge of a row of flat planks in front of the shack. "Well, I'll be," she said. "Look at what the cat dragged in. Come on, girls. It looks like we got us the makings of a real hootenanny."

Responding to that were the rest of the whores who'd been lounging in and around the shack. They wore their profession the way a lawman wore his badge. A couple of the women had loose blouses thrown over them, which they didn't even bother to button up. The rest simply wore dirty slips that only covered them from the waist down.

"Set my partners up with some entertainment," Smalls said. "And some whiskey for my new friends here."

"What about you, Tommy?" the redhead asked as she rubbed herself between her legs. "I kept it nice and warm for you."

Smalls climbed down from his saddle and eyed the whore as if she was a cut of fine meat. "I'll be right there, honey. This won't take long."

Mark looked over to Joey and gave a quick nod. Tightening his grip on his reins, he said, "That's fine, but we should really be—"

Reaching up to grab hold of Mark's elbow, Smalls pulled him down so quickly that Mark was barely able to get one leg out of the stirrup and onto the ground. "Nonsense!" Smalls bellowed. "Least I can do is give you boys a drink. Besides, Vin don't like it much when someone refuses our hospitality."

Vincent had one arm around a skinny topless woman with pasty skin and scraggly blond hair. Even so, he had his eyes on Mark and his other arm hanging down close to his holstered .38.

Since John, the third gunman, was also waiting to see what the next move was to be, Mark struggled to get disentangled from his other stirrup and said, "Come on, Joey. Let's not pass up a free drink."

"That's the spirit!" Smalls said as he roughly slapped

Mark on the shoulder. "Come on over here and tell me about this deal you had to offer."

"Oh, right. The deal."

As much as Mark had wanted to bolt out of that dung heap as quickly as his horse could carry him, he knew he would have been lucky to make it ten feet before Smalls and his partners opened fire. Now Mark wasn't even able to take a step in the wrong direction without Smalls's iron grip shoving him toward one of the darker shacks.

"Come on, boy," Smalls said to Joey. "That pussy'll be right here when you get back."

Joey climbed down from his saddle. A tall woman with darker skin approached him with a pleasant smile on her face. She held that smile when she looked at Joey's horse and led it away as if it had somehow been handed over to her for good.

"I'll be honest with ya," Smalls said. "You might've been a bit of help in town, but you seemed useless on the trail. You men fancy yerselves as bad men?"

"Sure as hell do," Joey grunted as he stepped into the dark shack.

The shack was something of a saloon, since there was liquor being served from behind a sorry excuse for a bar. Although the men who were already there looked like they had one foot in the grave, they still had enough steam left in their engines to laugh at what Joey had just said.

Smalls was laughing too. He kept right on laughing as he drew his pistol, thumbed back the hammer and jammed the barrel up under Mark's chin. "I like men with gumption, so I'll tell you what. Pitch your deal and I'll let you know if I like it."

"And . . . if you do?" Mark asked.

"Then I don't decorate this here ceiling with your brains."

Mark tried to nod, but found it difficult considering the placement of Smalls's gun. "There's some gold being held by a farmer."

"Huh?"

"That's right. Gold. Lots of it. I saw a chunk as big as your head being stashed in his barn."

"Bullshit," Smalls grunted. He leaned forward and lowered his voice to a fierce whisper. "How stupid you think I am?"

"It's there. I saw it," Mark insisted. "But there's someone there protecting it. A gunman by the looks of him. He got a look at us, so he'll know we're coming."

"Just one gunman and you couldn't get that gold yerselves?"

"The gunman and the farmer," Joey corrected.

Smalls laughed under his breath and nodded. "Right. A gunman and a farmer. Come to think of it, I could see how you two might get chased out of there. What's yer deal?"

Swallowing and pulling in a breath, Mark said, "I show you where the gold is. We go get it and we split it up."

"My men'll be doing most of the work, so we'll get most of the gold," Smalls said.

"Fine. I'll be happy with taking one of the women there for myself. She's mine and nobody else touches her."

Smalls let out a slow sigh through a slack jaw. Finally, he lowered his pistol. "Fine. Take us there and we'll get the gold. If it's there, I can buy all the whores I want. If it ain't, I kill you both after taking that woman you fancy so much. Deal?"

"Sure," Mark said as if he had any other choice. "It's a deal."

THIRTY-NINE

Clint felt as if he'd only just fallen onto his bed in Wes's house when the door creaked open and the farmer stuck his head inside.

"That you, Clint?" Wes asked.

Straining to sit up, Clint replied, "More or less."

"I heard the bank in town was robbed."

"You heard right."

"See why I didn't trust that place?"

"Yeah, Wes. You made the right call on that one."

"You still want to sleep?"

Clint filled his lungs with cool morning air and wondered if his answer would actually make a difference in what came next. "It'd be nice."

After a pause, Wes nodded. "I'm making breakfast, so I'll let you rest until it's done."

"Don't bother," Clint said as he swung his feet over the side of the bed. "I'm awake now. Are the others waiting for me?"

"Nope. Tina and Lynn are already working."

Considering how tired he was and what he'd done to get that way, Clint could only imagine how Tina was feeling. When he did imagine it, he couldn't help but grin. "What are they working on?" he asked as he walked down the short hallway to the modest kitchen.

Wes was already standing at the stove and tending to some bacon frying in a skillet. "They're helping me hide the gold."

"They know about it?"

Wes shook his head. "Nope. Far as they know, they're just fixing up the mess I left in that pumpkin patch. Tina was always after me to plant some cucumbers, so now's as good a time as any. It shouldn't be long before that ground looks good as new and nobody'll suspect there's much of anything there besides some seeds."

"What about the rest of what we talked about?"

"You mean turning my farm into a damned fort?" Wes asked.

Clint helped himself to some coffee and lifted the hot brew to his mouth. "That's not exactly what we talked about, but we're thinking alike."

"You want me to prepare this home to fight off some kind of attack," Wes grunted. "Sounds like a fort to me."

The coffee was just good enough to stay down when Clint drank it and just strong enough to shake the remaining tiredness from his bones. "The two men who came by the last time have joined up with some dangerous men. Real killers, as a matter of fact."

Wes looked up from the skillet and asked, "Like them bank robbers?"

Clint nodded. "Those are the ones. You get pretty good news up here on this farm."

"The whole damn town and everyone else within ten miles heard about that bank robbery. Since Thickett don't normally see them kind of men, it ain't much to figure out. So Mark had a hand in robbing the bank and killing the locals?"

"Mark shot one of them, but I don't think he was there to rob the bank."

"How can you be sure?"

"Because I crossed paths with the robbers on our way into town," Clint replied. "Mark was with them, but he looked like he was being dragged along. Besides, I've seen enough of Mark and his goal to know they don't have what it takes to rob a bank. A candy store, maybe, but not a bank."

The old farmer laughed as he divided up the bacon onto plates that were already holding a healthy serving of eggs. "From what Lynn told me about them, I'd say you were right. Mark always struts around like a bad man, but don't do nothin' more than talk to back it up. Talk and slap around a woman, that is. I hope the asshole gets what's coming to him."

"Don't worry about that," Clint said as he picked up a plate and walked over to the table. "They always get what's coming to them."

FORTY

Clint and Wes had talked a bit about what could be done to defend his farm in case anyone came back to try and claim the gold for themselves. At the time, Clint had been thinking more along the lines of getting the farmer ready to fight sometime after Clint had moved on. Now, however, it seemed they might be getting visitors a lot sooner.

The first thing on Clint's agenda had been to move the gold. That was done.

The second thing was for Wes to be able to get his daughter and Lynn to safety if they happened to be there when something happened. Since Tina had grown up on the farm and Lynn had spent a good amount of time there as a child, both of them knew plenty of places in which to hide.

Of course, getting either of the two strong-willed women to hide was going to be another task in itself.

The final of Clint's suggestions had been to try and get Wes prepared to convince armed men to leave his property when they were looking for gold. Although the farmer was more than willing to fight for his land and family, Clint was hoping to make sure Wes lived through the fight. That would involve a bit more strategy.

"Did you place those guns where I told you?" Clint asked as he walked between the barn and the stable.

Wes walked alongside him with his hands stuffed deeply into his pockets. "I don't got more'n a few old rifles and a shotgun."

"That's all you need. Did you place them where I told you?" Sensing the hackles on the old man's neck rising, Clint rephrased that: "Did you place them where I asked?"

"Yeah, but I don't have much by way of ammunition."

"That would have been good to know before Tina and I went into town."

"Well, pardon the hell out of me! Maybe I was a bit more concerned with a strange man riding off with my daughter."

Clint looked over to Wes and asked, "You didn't save one of those shotguns for me, did you?"

The old farmer cracked half a smile and shrugged. "Tina's old enough to do what she pleases. Hell, she's had a mind to do whatever she wants since she was a child."

Having already trod this ground, Clint let the old man simmer down before continuing the conversation. He did, however, manage to steer Wes away from the stable.

"I didn't see much," Clint said. "But I do know that Mark and his friend were with the gunmen who were riding out of town."

"Tina told me you were on the posse to go after those fellas."

"Sure, but that didn't turn out too good. I was lucky to keep some of the posse from getting themselves killed. Normally, I'd track the gunmen down myself."

"And why not this time?" Wes asked.

"Because I think I have a pretty good idea of where they'll be headed."

"You said Mark saw my gold?"

Clint nodded.

"And you think he'd tell the killers about it?"

"Seeing as how badly he got chased off the last couple of times he tried to come after me, I think so."

The old farmer looked up at his stable and let his eyes wander back toward the barn. "Damn," he muttered.

"My thoughts exactly."

"You two trying to hide out while we do all the work around here?" Lynn asked as she walked up to Clint and Wes. She wore a brown dress that showed the wear of working in the dirt for the last couple hours. She pulled a set of gloves off her hands and held onto them as she rubbed Wes on the shoulder.

"Clint thinks there may be trouble," Wes explained.

"If you're worried about Mark and Joey, I wouldn't be so sure," Lynn said. "They like to talk a whole lot more than they like to fight."

"Have they ever done any robberies?" Clint asked.

Lynn laughed a bit and shook her head. "You mean like that bank robbery in town? If they were in on that, it wasn't their idea. Mark used to talk about robbing eleven dollars from a general store. Actually, he used to brag about it."

"Nothing more than that?"

She shook her head without a moment's hesitation.

"What about shooting anyone?" Clint asked. "He's taken plenty of shots at me."

"And he didn't hit much of anything," Lynn replied. "That's Mark Rowlett for you."

Even though Clint shared a bit of Lynn's laughter, his smile slipped some when he asked, "How far do you think he'd go to get you back?"

That caused her smile to slip as well. Taking a deep breath and holding up her chin, she told him, "Just about anything he could. He may not know much about how to treat a lady, but Mark sure doesn't like letting one go."

"Would it surprise you to think he might have joined up with the bank robbers if it meant using them to come back here and take you out of here?"

Some of the color drained from Lynn's face, but her voice didn't waver. "Not in the least," she said.

"Then I need to have a word with you and Tina."

"Tina knows all about Mark, Clint. I've told her plenty."

"It's not about him," Clint said. "I'd like to see how well you two can handle a gun."

FORTY-ONE

When he'd first arrived, Mark thought there was no way in hell he'd want to buy what the whores at that trading post were selling. Once he'd managed to get Smalls and his men to work for him, however, Mark was much more ready to celebrate.

Along with the whiskey, Smalls handed over a few coins to a short woman who was missing half her teeth. Mark allowed himself to be dragged to the woman's room, hoping that he could close his eyes and still enjoy the next few minutes.

"That's it, darlin'," the whore grunted as she straddled him and pumped her hips. "Keep it on just like that."

Mark moaned once and trembled slightly as a smile drifted onto his face. "Damn. That was pretty good," he sighed.

The whore was still pumping, but she slowed down once she felt that Mark was no longer moving. Suddenly, she looked at him as if she'd seen warts spring up from every pore of his body. "What? You mean that's it?"

"That's plenty. You did your job."

Letting out a disgusted breath, she climbed off and

pulled her slip down to cover herself. "Damn, that's got to be the sorriest piece of fucking I ever seen."

Mark hiked up his britches and slapped the whore across her mouth. At that moment, he realized just how much he missed Lynn. Since the whore didn't move, he slapped her again. "Get those legs open," he said. "I want another poke."

Rubbing her cheek with the back of one hand, the whore started to pull up her slip and open her legs. As soon as Mark was close enough, she brought one of her legs straight up to slam Mark directly in the groin. "I'll be damned if I'll let an asshole like you lay another damn hand on me. Besides," she added while stomping past him to the door, "you only paid for one."

The pain that went through Mark's groin felt like a hot poker was slipping around inside of him. When he let out a shaky breath, he thought he might have pissed himself. Mark reached down to check, but realized he'd at least been spared that indignity.

"I been to these whores plenty of times and I've seen plenty of things," John said from the doorway. "But I ain't never seen something as funny as that."

Mark was about to ask just how much the gunman had seen. On second thought, he decided it was just as good if he didn't know.

"Tommy and Vin want to get moving," John said. "Soon as you find your other nut, you'd best come outside and lead the way."

Nodding as he struggled to his feet, Mark thought about how much better Lynn was than one of those whores. He missed her and was anxious to get her back. When Joey's voice cut in on his thoughts, Mark almost took a swing at him.

"These ladies aren't all that bad," Joey said. "Sounds like there was some hootin' and hollerin' in here."

"Just collect our things so we can get the hell out of this shit hole."

In the few minutes it took for Mark to get outside, he'd managed to walk a straight line without wincing too badly. Judging by the grins on all three of the gunmen's faces, however, Mark wasn't about to fool anyone no matter how straight he walked.

Just as he thought he might get away from the trading post with a shred of dignity intact, Mark heard Smalls shout to him.

"You gonna be riding sidesaddle, boy?"

Mark thought of a few nasty ways to answer the question, but was discouraged by the sight of all the gunmen who seemed a bit too anxious to knock him down a few pegs. So Mark grinned and shook his head.

"Not this time," he said. "It'll take more than that to put a dent in me. Are we going to sweep through that farm?"

"You're gonna show me the gold," Smalls replied.

Mark looked around and noticed that Smalls was the only man on horseback. The other two had taken up positions on either side of Joey.

"You didn't think we'd just thunder off with guns blazing on your say-so, did you?" Smalls asked.

"Actually, I thought we'd—"

"Just take me close enough to get a look at it," Smalls interrupted. "Then we'll figure a good way to get it out of there."

Mark forced himself to seem like he was in control when he pointed out, "But there's too much that can go wrong. What if the farmer sees us? What if we run into the law along the way?"

"That posse was made up of a bunch of tenderfeet," Smalls grunted. "And I ain't about to worry myself about one farmer, neither."

"I told you there was another gunman there too. What if

he's there? Wouldn't you rather go in with all your men behind you?"

"Not when we could be riding into some kind of trap. Me and my boys here got prices on our heads that'd make you a rich man. We've had plenty of assholes try to bait us into some corner or another just so they could take an easy shot at us. Then there's the chance that you could be making up the story about this gold just to save your own ass."

Shaking his head, Mark sputtered, "I'm not making it up. I swear I saw it right there—"

Smalls stopped him with a raised hand and the cold hint of death in his eyes. "All I want is a look-see. If the gold's there, we'll come get the boys and haul it out of there. If there ain't no gold, well . . . I got a few things in mind that'll make getting kicked in the tobacco pouch seem downright pleasant. And if I'm not back with some good news, Vin and John will have some fun skinning your friend there."

Climbing into his saddle while fighting back a pained grimace, Mark said, "All right. Let's go."

FORTY-TWO

A shot blasted through the air and struck home loudly enough to be heard from a distance. Seeing that they'd dropped their target, the person behind the rifle let out a victorious cheer.

"All right, all right," Clint said. "You hit a bottle. No need to celebrate just yet."

Lynn straightened up and held the rifle propped against her hip as if she was posing for a photographer. "Considering that's only after a few lessons, I think it's more than enough cause to celebrate."

"See if you can spot the other target I set up for you," Clint replied.

Lowering herself back down so she was lying on her stomach, Lynn stretched her legs out behind her and settled in behind her rifle. The constant flow of wind caught her hair and a piece of her skirt, ruffling both but not disturbing either too much.

Clint sat beside her on the roof of the house. His legs dangled over the side and he used one hand to keep his hat from flying off.

"So," Lynn said as she sighted along the top of her rifle

and slowly searched the field in front of her. "You've been spending a lot of time with Tina."

"Yep."

"She and I have always been close. One thing that bothers me, though . . ." After being still for a second, Lynn pulled the trigger and sent a single shot into the field. The shot was followed by the sound of shattering glass. "She always goes after any man who I spend more than an hour with."

Clint had been watching the bottle he'd placed in the field and was genuinely impressed that Lynn had found it and hit it so quickly. "Sounds like something you two should work out. Nice shot, by the way."

Lynn looked up at him for a few moments before grinning. "I've seen some men squirm when I bring that up."

"Well, there's plenty worse things out there than two friends who squabble over things like that. Would either one of you try to steal a husband from the other?"

"No," Lynn replied quickly.

"Then that's all you need to know. Everything else is just bickering. If you don't like that about her, maybe you shouldn't be friends."

Lynn was still staring up at him for a while, as if she was mulling something over in her head. After settling her cheek against the rifle once more, she said, "We've come to an agreement about this very thing a long time ago. I just like to see how a man reacts when he hears about it."

"Why go through all that? Is it that much fun to see someone squirm?"

"Sometimes, yeah." With that, Lynn fired off another shot.

"There's no more bottles out there, you know."

Lynn was still grinning as she levered in another round. "The reason we bring this up with certain men is sort of . . . a test."

"Should I even ask what you're testing for?"

"To see if a fellow can handle both of us."

Clint looked down at her to see if she was kidding. Even though Lynn wasn't looking back at him, he could tell she knew she was being watched. He could also tell that she wasn't kidding.

"My imagination is running wild," Clint said as he shifted his gaze out toward the field.

Lynn fired another shot and levered in another round. "When all this is over, maybe we could celebrate."

"Just us two, or . . . ?"

Allowing the question to hang in the air, Lynn fired a round into the field. This time, however, she hit something. A single crow flew up from the spot where the bullet had landed. Lynn levered in a round, sighted down the barrel and fired a shot.

Clint let out a low whistle as he watched the crow spin in midair and drop to the ground. "I didn't even see that one hiding down there. Very impressive."

"Thank you," Lynn replied as she extended her arm so Clint could help her up.

"Seems like you've got plenty of hidden talents."

"Play your cards right," she said with a wink, "and some more of 'em won't stay hidden too much longer."

As he helped Lynn climb down from the roof, Clint had a hard time focusing on the steps he was taking. His mind was elsewhere, sifting through the many wonderful possibilities that had arisen during their target practice.

At least some of those possibilities had to do with Lynn's marksmanship.

FORTY-THREE

It was early evening and Clint was getting restless. He wasn't the only one. Wes, Tina and Lynn were feeling the same way. Fixing and eating supper had given them all something to do, but that didn't hold them over for long. Eventually, Clint found himself with Wes riding the perimeter of the farm.

"You think Tina's going to be able to hold her own?" Clint asked.

"Hell, yes," the farmer replied proudly. "She's always been a fine shot. I taught her myself when she was a girl. Lynn too."

"Yeah. I found that out a while ago. What about you? How are you holding up?"

"Strangely enough, I wish those assholes would take a run at me sooner rather than later. If they don't come soon, does that mean I'm supposed to live with a knot in my gut for years to come?"

"If they don't come soon," Clint replied, "I doubt there'll be a problem. I'd give it a few days to a week at the most. Anything past that is probably beyond the limit of the killers' patience."

"Let's hope so."

As if answering the old man's wish, a shot was fired in the distance. Both Wes and Clint looked that way and then looked at each other.

"That came from the house," Wes said.

Although the farmer got his horse moving first, Clint had no trouble overtaking him. Eclipse raced forward and reached the house in no time. Clint pulled back on the reins before getting there and then motioned for Wes to do the same. The farmer slowed, but looked too anxious to keep still for long.

"Until we see who's shooting at what, we shouldn't just run into anything," Clint said.

Wes nodded, but didn't look happy about it. He seemed to feel a little better once he got his rifle in his hands. "I'll head toward the house and you circle around the barn. Sound good to you?"

"Sounds great. Let's go." With that, Clint flicked the reins with one hand and filled the other with his modified Colt. Eclipse responded to every subtle shift of Clint's legs or feet, moving as if he could read Clint's thoughts.

"They're over there, Wes!" Lynn shouted from the house.

Clint couldn't see where Lynn might have been pointing, but he could sure see the two figures rushing away from the barn. As soon as one of the figures leaned out to look back at the house, another shot was fired at him.

"God damn!" Smalls shouted as he pulled his head back and ran a little faster toward the stable.

As he steered to cut the men off, Clint sifted through various calculations in his head. He estimated things like how much he was moving in the saddle and how much farther it would be before he was in the Colt's range. He didn't have to wonder how long it would take for the other men to hear him coming, since both of them looked directly at him.

Clint recognized one of them as Mark Rowlett. Although the other wasn't wearing a duster, Clint was fairly

certain he was one of the bank robbers who had been
chased out of Thickett. That was more than enough for
Clint to raise his gun and take the first shot that presented
itself.

The Colt bucked against Clint's palm and sent a shot
past Mark's head. Both men raised their hands and fired
right back at him. Eclipse didn't need to feel more than
half a nudge from Clint to know what to do. The Darley
Arabian turned sharply from the gunfire and tore away.

Clint twisted in the saddle and fired at the two men
again. Both of them had already ducked behind the stable.
The bank robber was even taking the time to line up his
shot.

Cursing under his breath, Clint pulled on the reins to
make Eclipse turn sharply around and change direction before Smalls drew a bead on him. Another shot hissed a few
yards away from him and might have drawn blood if Clint
hadn't made the sudden move. Unfortunately, it took another couple of seconds for Eclipse to turn around again.

"Go on!" Smalls shouted.

Both Smalls and Mark ran from the stable and into the
nearby field. Their horses waited there behind a few trees.
Even though Clint had seen the animals there, he hadn't
had much time to do anything about it. Keeping his body
low over the stallion's neck, he got Eclipse racing toward
the two men.

Before making it to the field, Smalls turned his back to
the trees and kept moving toward them using a backward
shuffle. He wore a wide smile on his face as he raised both
arms to take aim with a pistol in each hand.

Clint pulled sharply on the reins and fired a shot at
Smalls, hoping it might be enough to keep the approaching
storm of lead away for another second or two. But Smalls
didn't even flinch at the incoming round. Instead, he started
pulling his triggers and firing both guns at Clint.

Firing reflexively, Clint put one bullet into Smalls's

arm. Even that wasn't enough to back the other man down. Just as the incoming bullets got closer to hitting Clint, another shot was fired from the house.

That shot sparked against the gun in Smalls's right hand and forced him to turn tail and race for his horse.

Clint glanced at the house and saw Lynn wave at him from the roof. He didn't know how she'd managed to get up there so quickly, but he reminded himself to thank her for it when he got back. For the moment, however, Clint had his hands full.

He wasn't about to let Mark get away from him again, so Clint fired a few more times at the trees and snapped the reins so Eclipse could close the distance between them.

Within seconds after Mark and Smalls stopped shooting, they were in their saddles and racing away from the trees. They were racing away from the house, as well, and heading into one of Wes's fields.

Putting Eclipse on a straight course, Clint gripped the reins in his teeth and used both hands to quickly reload the Colt. It wasn't the safest way to go about the task, but it sure brought a smile to his face as he closed the distance between himself and the fleeing gunmen.

FORTY-FOUR

"Where the hell did those two come from?" Wes asked as he ran to his front porch.

Tina stepped outside carrying a shotgun. "I thought I saw something moving and Lynn spotted them poking around the barn. She took a shot at them and spooked them before they got inside."

"So they didn't make it into the barn?" Wes asked.

"I don't think so. I went to get the shotgun, and Lynn climbed up to the roof like we agreed if there was any trouble. I think she might have hit one of them from up there."

Wes looked his daughter over quickly and let out his breath when he saw she wasn't hurt. "We'd better all get to our spots like we talked about. This might be what we were preparing for."

"I swear that gold is in there!" Mark hollered as he furiously whipped his horse with the reins. "If we could've gotten into that barn, you would've seen for yourself. You gotta believe me!"

Still wearing the grin that had been on his face since the shooting started, Smalls fired one more shot over his shoulder and looked back to Mark. "You can stop the cryin'. I believe you."

For a moment, Mark was more focused on Smalls than on the man who was chasing them. "You do?"

"Sure I do. With that many guns guarding the place, there's gotta be somethin' worth having in that barn. There sure as hell is more than just some damn bales of hay. Having a chunk of gold in there sounds about right to me."

"So do we go get the others?" Mark asked. "Or should we come back later?"

Another shot was fired from behind them, which hissed through the air directly between them. Mark pulled away so quickly that he nearly fell from his saddle. Smalls, on the other hand, casually checked over his shoulder as if looking for a sign of rain.

"If we wait, those farmers will just find some more guns to guard that place with," Smalls said. "Or they'll move the gold. We'll head back and catch 'em when they think we're runnin'."

"Just us?"

"Hell, no! I got a little surprise for them farmers."

Clint snapped the Colt shut with a flick of his wrist. He kept the gun in hand while taking hold of the reins. The field was flat, but there were plenty of tall crops and the occasional scarecrow in his line of sight to give the two men in front of him a little cover. Clint didn't know what the crops were, but he sure could have gotten a better shot without them in his way.

He urged Eclipse into a row between the tall stalks and was about to close the gap even more when he saw another group of horses converge on the two in front of him. As soon as both groups met up, they turned around to face Clint head-on.

Knowing a bad spot when he saw one, Clint followed suit and made a direction change of his own. Rather than head straight back to the barn, he circled around to the left and hung on as the stalks whipped at him from both sides.

Now that Eclipse was no longer running straight down one of the rows in between the stalks, it wasn't so easy to build up speed. It was a lot easier, however, to disappear from view as both groups of gunmen started firing toward Clint.

"Glad to see you boys could make it," Smalls shouted at Vin and John, who rode on either side of Joey.

John tipped his hat and replied, "All we needed to do was keep this one quiet while we followed you two."

"What about the gold?" Vincent asked. "Is it there?"

"There's somethin' valuable in that barn," Smalls replied excitedly. "And it'll belong to us when we ride out of here."

With that, Smalls snapped his reins and led the charge onto the Petrowski farm.

FORTY-FIVE

Clint raced back toward the house and circled around to the front. Since he'd managed to get out of their sights with his last couple of turns, he was able to work his way to the gate directly in front of the farmhouse. Hopefully, everyone else had had enough time to get to the spots they'd all practiced.

As soon as Clint bolted through the gate, he held his breath and prayed that nobody would take a panicked shot at him. No shots came, so he kept riding toward the barn. He didn't make it there before the riders cleared the field behind him.

Smalls led the way and fired his pistol while standing up in his stirrups. He shouted like a crazed barbarian and thundered straight toward the barn.

Vincent and John were close behind Smalls, and they rode toward the house. That path also put them in the clear, which set them up almost as well as a pair of bottles in a field.

Lynn's first shot caught John in the shoulder. It wasn't fatal, but it hit with more than enough force to knock him off his horse. Her second shot came soon after, but hissed through the air past Vincent's head.

John hit the ground on his side and spat all the air from

his lungs in one pained grunt. It was a struggle to get to his feet, but once he did he immediately started running toward the barn. He was about three paces from the front barn doors when a petite figure leaned out of the small square window that opened from the stable's loft.

With the shotgun already against her shoulder, Tina sighted along the barrels and pulled both triggers. The impact knocked her back into the loft, but she sent enough buckshot into the air to cut John down where he stood.

Several pellets hit John in the legs and back. Those, combined with the wounds he'd already taken, ended his run right then and there.

Vincent fired up toward the house's roof, but hit nothing more than a few shingles and an attic window. When he heard the shotgun, he turned in that direction while swinging his pistol around as well. He still couldn't see anyone to shoot at, which brought a mix of anger and confusion to his face.

"Hey, boy," Wes said as he emerged from the house's front door.

Vincent turned and took aim at the old farmer. He pulled his trigger at the same time that Wes pulled his.

Both men drew blood and both men hit the ground hard.

As soon as he'd ridden around to the back of the barn, Smalls jumped down from his saddle and ran for the rear door. "This the spot, Mark?"

Mark and Joey had been sure to come in behind the other three, so they'd only just arrived. Mark nodded, but couldn't get his eyes to stay focused on one spot for very long. "Yeah, but that other one should be right—"

"Right here," Clint said as he pulled open the barn door. Eclipse was behind him and off to the right side where he could watch things unfold from a fairly safe distance.

"Hand over the gold and we'll leave in peace," Smalls said.

Clint scowled and looked at Smalls as if he'd heard a bad joke. "Too late to make that promise, don't you think?"

"All right then. How about you hand over the gold and I let you and all these farmers live?"

"I don't think you've got the firepower to back that up," Clint replied.

Smalls looked around and then waited for a few seconds, but all he heard was the thunder of the previous gunshots rolling farther away. "I got all I need right here," Smalls said as he tightened his fist around his pistol.

That subtle bit of motion was enough to make Clint's entire body tense.

Smalls reacted to that by reflexively lowering his arm before he got himself shot.

"There's no gold in here," Clint said. "Take a look for yourself."

"It's right there under those rags," Mark shouted.

Stepping sideways toward the little pile of rags in the corner, Smalls tapped it with his toe and kicked some of the rags aside. All he found underneath was straw and a wooden floor.

"There was gold, I swear!" Mark groaned.

Gritting his teeth, Smalls let out a snarl that eventually formed into some words. "There's something you're all guarding and I aim to find it. Even if I have to burn this whole fucking place to the ground!"

As he uttered that vow, Smalls brought up his gun to make good on it.

Clint's arm snapped up and he aimed the modified Colt as if he was pointing his finger. He pulled the trigger once, which was enough to send a single round through Smalls's skull.

Even before Smalls had dropped, Mark was rushing into the barn. "It's here, goddammit. I know it's here!"

"Just leave, Mark," Lynn said as she stepped through the front door of the barn. Her face and dress were smudged from climbing up and down from the roof, but she still looked good enough to capture all of Mark's attention.

"You're coming back with me," Mark said as he rushed toward her.

Clint shifted his aim and thumbed back his hammer. Sure enough, the metallic click from the pistol was enough to stop Mark in his tracks.

Still, Mark reached out for Lynn and locked his eyes upon her.

As she walked past Clint, Lynn patted him on the shoulder. "It's all right. I need to have another word with him."

"I thought I saw Wes get shot," Clint said.

"He did, but it's just a flesh wound. Tina's tending to him right now."

"You probably should let me take care of these two."

"No," Lynn insisted. "I need to finish this."

Clint let her get closer to him, but kept his Colt aimed at Mark's chest. One stern glare was all it took to get Joey to drop his gun and raise his arms.

"I'm not going with you, Mark," Lynn said. "Not now. Not ever."

"But I did all this for you. All of it!"

"Like shooting at my friends and coming here to kill these good people?"

"Yeah," Mark replied. "For you!"

"You're a sick son of a bitch," Lynn spat.

Mark pulled back his hand and snarled, "Dirty bitch!" He got through half of a swing intended to knock her head from her shoulders before Lynn's rifle went off and dropped him to his knees.

As much as he wanted to scream, Mark didn't have enough breath to make a sound. All he could do was lie on his side, curl into a ball and grab at the bloody pulp of his groin.

Taking advantage of the cold sweat that had broken out on Joey's brow, Clint said, "If you spread any more lies about there being gold on this farm, you'll get the same as your friend."

"I ain't never seen that gold," Joey stammered. "Please just take me to a jail far away from her."

"I think that can be arranged."

Clint then walked over to Lynn and moved her away so he could take Mark's gun.

The look in Lynn's eyes was cold and distant as she said, "I did the bastard a favor. He never knew what to do with that thing of his anyway."

Watch for

UNDER A TURQUOISE SKY

312th novel in the exciting GUNSMITH
series from Jove

Coming in December!

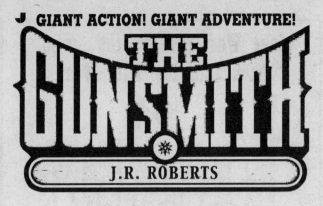

GIANT ACTION! GIANT ADVENTURE!

THE GUNSMITH

J.R. ROBERTS

LITTLE SURESHOT AND THE WILD WEST SHOW (GUNSMITH GIANT #9)
9780515138511

DEAD WEIGHT (GUNSMITH GIANT #10)
9780515140286

RED MOUNTAIN (GUNSMITH GIANT #11)
9780515142068

THE KNIGHTS OF MISERY (GUNSMITH GIANT #12)
9780515143690

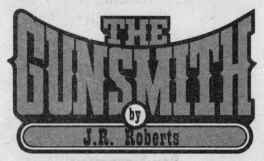

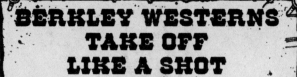